The Skipper Goes West

Book Two of 'The Skipper' Series

Mark Tissington

Wandering Tree Publications Limited

Dedicated to Matthew, our missing man.
You will always be loved.

Chapter One

London, Euston Station

Euston Station smelled of burning coal and ashes. The iron grid work supporting the roof frequently disappeared in clouds of grey steam as they readied locomotives. The noise of conversations, yelling, and guard's whistles were a constant background.

Two men in trilbys and dark suits leaned against a pillar, smoking. They watched a porter wheeling a black metal box on a barrow. The younger of the two tensed as two men ran up behind the porter, laughing. The porter turned, looking shocked as they spoke to him, then smiled and turned around toward the Liverpool train.

The dark suits glanced at each other and walked toward the train, then stopped. Four capable looking men had disembarked from the train and stood across their path.

They had their hands inside their jackets and held their gaze on the dark suits.

A dark-haired man with a clipped moustache stepped between the four men and approached. He was dressed in a grey suit and homburg hat, and was holding his jacket open to reveal a Webley service pistol on a lanyard.

'Gentlemen, we've cleared the area behind you in case we need to use violence, but I'd rather we didn't. Please put your weapons on the floor in front of you.'

He glanced left and right as his men formed a half circle, two on each side.

The dark suits carefully placed a pistol and a nasty-looking dagger on the grimy floor. At which point, the man in the homburg smiled as one of his men scooped up the weapons and patted the clothing of the two prisoners.

'Good show. Now if you'll come this way, we'll go and find some privacy. Oh Lord! My manners. Please do call me Captain McDonald.'

The Skipper and Arthur leaned back against their settee in the Mariner's Rest Inn. They had taken a table next to a window, which Gerald had left open to counter the sultry heat. Before each man was a pint of Sturdy Mariner, the best pint of bitter in Yorkshire and therefore, of course, the world.

Arthur watched dust motes dancing in a bar of sunlight

which lanced through the window. It was like watching minuscule creatures going about their lives being buffeted by huge forces beyond their control. A small gust of summer breeze or a passing person made them swirl and dance, tiny stars in the sunbeam. Looking over at his friend and employer, he remembered it was the Skipper who protected himself and the rest of the crew from at least some forces affecting their own lives. His Majesty's Trawler White Nab, on which Arthur served as First Mate, was a happy and very effective ship. They were nominally part of the Royal Naval Patrol Service, escorting convoys and carrying out anti-Submarine patrols, but they also served as a support for the Secret Intelligence Service, covertly dropping or collecting assets as required.

The Skipper took a long draught from his beer and smiled.

'This is the life, Arthur.'

'It is, Skipper, it certainly is.'

As they spoke, two soldiers noisily arrived and leaned against the bar. The Skipper's eyes narrowed, but he said nothing. They resumed their chat, ignoring the extra volume until the words, 'This beer is like cat's pee!' rang out.

The Skipper slowly rose and strolled to the bar. Gerald, the landlord of the inn and the man who brewed the beer, reached behind him toward a cricket trophy board. He carefully removed the bat, which appeared to be secured, but was in fact their favourite weapon against loutish behaviour.

As the Skipper neared the two men they looked up and, seeing the golden stripes on his RNR officer's jacket, fell silent.

'Gentlemen; the regulars here are enjoying a restful afternoon drinking what is, in truth, an excellent pint of best bitter. So may I suggest you keep your voices down, your comments to yourself, or just bugger off?'

The two men stood at attention, apologising profusely with lots of 'sir' thrown in. The Skipper looked disappointed as they drained their glasses and left, still apologising. Gerald slid the cricket bat, 'Excalibur,' back onto its mount and grinned at the Skipper.

'There's no fun for you anymore Skipper, not since you got all that string on your arms!'

'I know Gerald, I'm going to have to go into nets to practise my swing at this rate.' The Skipper returned to his table.

A voice from the door made the Skipper and Arthur abruptly turn.

'A pint for me please Gerald and another for these two reprobates!'

Captain Horace McDonald paid for the drinks and strolled over to their table. The Skipper and Arthur both rose as he approached.

'I understand that many Yorkshire folk have Scandinavian blood in them. I suppose this may explain your conquering spirit and predilection for pillage?'

Arthur and the Skipper laughed, shaking his hand.

'What brings you to these parts, sir?' the Skipper asked.

'Well, I really wanted a quick chat with you chaps but I hear they shot you up a little?'

'Nothing major sir, our very first convoy escort after refitting and a blessed e-boat peppered us in the dark. Usual tactic, sit inshore of the swept channel, wait until we pass then start up and play havoc! The funnel and flying bridge suffered some damage, and one boat was wrecked, but he only got one pass. We started responding with the twelve pounder and an old V class destroyer got into him, so he fled. The yard couldn't get her in for a week, but they say she'll be ready in two or three days, if that's any use?'

'Definitely Skipper; if we can find somewhere quiet after our pint I'll tell you what I can.'

Arthur stood, 'Gerald has a function room upstairs, sir. Shall I ask if we can use it?'

'First rate, we can sample the beer and hold a briefing at the same time.' McDonald smiled.

A few minutes later, they sat in the centre of the empty room. McDonald had left the door slightly ajar.

'Can't afford ears against doors, I'm afraid. Right chaps; first some background information. This is beyond top secret for all sorts of reasons, so we have to take incredible precautions on this job. A very senior scientist, Sir Henry Tizard, is currently in the United States on a mission to promote technological collaboration between the US and ourselves during this war. It is sensitive because, as you know, the US is currently neutral, and in fact there are many over there who are against them entering the war at all. Despite that, our Prime Minister believes they will ultimately ally themselves with Great Britain and declare war on the Axis powers. The Tizard mission is intended to offer technology exchange and to tap into the enormous manufacturing capacity which the Americans possess. Sir Henry flew ahead and his team followed a few days ago with some example technology. All clear so far?'

The Skipper nodded, 'Absolutely, sir.'

McDonald nodded, 'Good. Anyway, we captured two enemy agents in London who were trying to intercept the box of equipment intended for Sir Henry. Someone in our sister organisation, the Security Service, got wind of a network of agents being established over here and we helped with surveillance. It turns out, from what we learned, that they created this network either to infiltrate the mission, or to steal the example technology which is being taken over there. We would never have discovered the network had more time been available for the enemy to prepare, but their haste led to errors and we caught them red-handed, trying to filch the box of goodies being sent to show the Americans.'

The Skipper frowned, 'Can you say how the Nazis found out about the mission? It must have been kept under wraps, I would have thought?'

'It was a low-level clerk at the Air Ministry with gambling debts. The Security Service try to filter the vulnerable out, but I'm afraid that every so often, one gets past them. Anyway, we are now aware how badly the Nazis want this technology themselves, so naturally the mission throws a spanner in the Nazi works. There's another piece of technology which the team want to show the Americans. We're not keen on them taking it by train and ship this time, so we want to take it to them using a trusted party with the means to cross the Atlantic quietly. I expect you can see where this is going, but this is also why we're involved past assisting with surveillance. This is getting goods into a neutral power's country which hostile agents would dearly love to intercept. So who's for a trip to the United States?'

The Skipper smiled, 'Of course, sir. Because they don't drink best bitter over there, we shall suffer for the cause, but will get this thingummy delivered.'

McDonald grinned, 'Good show, oh and no piracy this time Skipper!'

The Skipper's eyes widened, 'Sir! I resemble that remark!'

Chapter Two

51° 30′ 00″ N, 00° 7′ 59″ W

London, SIS Headquarters

Captain Horace McDonald sat in a slightly battered leather armchair in the office of his boss, Sir Peter Hayford. The bustle of Broadway, outside the large window, sounded muted, and the dominant sound in the room was the slow clunk of an enormous clock: the type often seen in railway station waiting rooms. McDonald, declining Sir Peter's proffered cigar, reclined in the armchair while Sir Peter, a tall, distinguished and imposing man, poured whisky from a decanter.

The scent of the spirit relaxed McDonald, and he started slightly as Sir Peter spoke.

'So Horace, how are we progressing with Operation Jasper?'

McDonald straightened himself, taking a deep breath.

'Painfully slowly, sir I'm afraid. Of the two agents we arrested, the British citizen knows nothing. His involvement seems to arise from having had a German mother and a life of thuggery. The German chap, however, is a professional. We are getting nothing from him directly, but by looking at what he won't answer and, more importantly, the answers we believe to be misdirections, I think the Nazis know nothing.'

Sir Peter thought for a second, then spoke in a low voice, 'Thin grounds upon which to hypothesise, don't you think?'

McDonald nodded, 'That's my concern too, sir. The only reason I voice it is the Air Ministry clerk who passed information to the Nazis fell apart under questioning from my chaps. He swears the only information he possessed was that a crate of sensitive equipment was to be shipped through Euston on the 14th, and we had classed this event as top secret. He also told them that his orders were to arrange transport, from an address provided by his boss to Euston Station. Obviously, he gave them the date. My men had him in fear of the noose and yet he stuck by this. I'd suspect he was minimising damage, except he actually wet himself during interrogation. I'm convinced he is telling the truth.'

Steepling his fingers, Sir Peter smiled, 'Poor chap! Yes, I'm inclined to agree with you. The Nazis fielded a pretty weak team, and if they really knew what was in the crate, I'd expect a more competent crew. So what next?'

'Well sir, I've got HMT White Nab lined up to join a west-bound convoy to Halifax. A member of Sir Henry's team will meet them and take delivery of the backup devices. Our chaps over there will provide discrete security cover, as an addition to the U.S. military escort, of course.'

Sir Peter leaned forward, 'Well now, that brings me to my next point. I had a long conversation with C this morning. He wants a senior officer to be in attendance when the goodies go over the pond and there's nobody I trust more than yourself. Would you nominate a deputy to take over any other caseload, please? You must fly over to the US in the next two or three days.'

McDonald's eyebrows came together slightly, 'Of course sir, I shall do that. May I ask why C feels this is necessary?'

It was Sir Peter's turn to frown, 'Protecting the PM's reputation, it seems. Apparently there was a lot of objection to Sir Henry's mission, a lot of politics, but the PM allowed it in the end, indeed, the government will no doubt claim it as their own in the event it succeeds. It would therefore be embarrassing to have to admit to our potential allies that we lost our own secret equipment, what?'

'You have a point sir, most definitely,' McDonald raised his glass, 'to success then!'

Sir Peter took a sip, then became serious.

'The thing is Horace, I've been speaking to a couple of senior figures in the FBI.'

McDonald put down his glass, 'And what became of that, sir?'

Nodding and thoughtful, Sir Peter replied, 'They are concerned about what they fear is a newly formed ring of Nazi spies in the United States. This arises from your heads-up to your FBI contact. Now, the intelligence they have is ambiguous. Some feel that it points to a ring being created in North America, while others believe the northern operation is about transmitting information back to Europe, with the actual espionage taking place in South America. If the first camp are correct, and factoring in your excellent intervention at Euston, well, the feeling is they may have another go at pilfering our equipment in the United States. Taking the political aspect on this side of the wide Atlantic into account, and considering the low-likelihood but high-consequence nature of a North American ring being mature enough to pull off an operation against the Tizard Mission, well, I'd rather have a capable man on the ground.'

McDonald pulled out his notebook and wrote for a short while, 'Sir, I wonder, could I retain the services of White Nab once she delivers the equipment? Perhaps a mobile operational base, one which can quickly get into international waters, might be an asset if certain scenarios play out. Again, this is insurance only.'

'Not a bad idea dear boy, yes, I'll approach the Admiralty and if they say no, I'll let the PM's personal secretary ring them.'

McDonald chuckled, 'Thank you, sir.'

Sir Peter beamed at his trusted subordinate, 'One last point on that subject, Horace. C assures me, and I don't doubt him, that there is no political element to his request to send someone. I rather indelicately suggested that the token British subject might become a scapegoat in the event the whole thing goes south. C has assured me that, if our American cousins try any such tactic, he will employ every trick of diplomacy to block it. In addition, he said this morning that he has secured a commitment from the nearest FBI office in Boston, Massachusetts, to provide support. He and I feel that a joint operation is less likely to result in any silliness in the event of a poor outcome.'

McDonald smiled, 'Very reassuring sir.'

Sir Peter glanced at the door and lowered his voice, 'On the subject of politics, I had our first clash of heads with our newest friends, the Special Operations Executive. I still think of them as our own Section D, I'm afraid. They made a bid for this operation, so I took the direct route and asked them to point out how this was sabotaging the enemy, setting Europe alight or helping resistance fighters; given that the US is a neutral power, and a potential ally. I'm told the PM's exact words to them were "Don't be bloody foolish" so I think we can lay that to rest! No doubt the skirmishes will continue over the boundaries of each organisation's remit.'

McDonald shook his head, 'Lord love office politics, sir. Where would we be without them?'

'Probably burying Herr Hitler already dear boy. You and I would be sipping schnapps in the headquarters of the Sicherheitsdienst by now, I suspect!

Chapter Three

54° 16' 59" N, 00° 23' 25" W

Scarborough North Riding

Mother smoothed down her apron, which was usually a bad sign, and fixed her son with an intense stare.

'You're going where?'

The Skipper resisted the urge to squirm, 'Canada, Mother, a place called Halifax in Nova Scotia, that's on their east coast.'

She glared at him, but he knew her knowledge of geography was sketchy and he wanted to avoid any idea he would be circumnavigating the globe.

Mavis, the love of his life, and also the torment of his soul, leaned on the doorjamb and smirked. He knew she was about to stir the fire.

'So you'll be gone for some time then, Reggie my love?'

The Skipper's eyes narrowed, and he braced for more of Mother's ire. In the same way as he was always 'the Skipper', most of Scarborough's old town knew her simply as 'Mother'. Such was her presence, linked to a big heart and a genuine fondness for her neighbours.

Mother fumed, as only she knew how, 'And precisely how long is 'some time' Reggie dear?'

Her arms were now folded, a sure sign that battle was about to be joined, so he picked his words carefully.

'Well, a week or so to cross the Atlantic, same to return, of course...'

Mother's eyes flared as she oozed sarcasm, 'Well, I never! Who'd have thought that?'

He decided that no response was the best option, 'After arriving, we're not really sure what will be required of us. Captain McDonald told me we might have to travel down to the United States, but he will brief us before we leave. As I've told Mavis, I shall send you the address for the fleet post office in Halifax, and I'll send a telegram in the event of anything urgent. How's that?'

'Well, it'll have to do, I suppose!'

The Skipper smiled, 'Good, now who would like some tea?'

Mother stood, winking at Mavis, 'He thinks he can buy us with tea, lass. What do you think of that?'

'Not much, Mother, not very much at all.'

The Skipper's heart shrank with the realisation that an unholy alliance had already formed. This almost certainly sealed his fate.

Later, as he walked Mavis uphill to her parent's house, her arm through his, he squeezed her hand, 'You mustn't worry my love, the sea is no more dangerous in the Atlantic than in the Arctic.'

She glanced up at him, 'I know Reggie, but it's no less dangerous and now it's full of submarines...' she tailed off.

He squeezed again, 'Well, we have a rack full of depth charges and an ASDIC operator who can hear a whale two miles away!'

She squeezed his hand back, 'Careful Reggie, "Pride goeth before destruction, and a haughty spirit before a fall" you know!'

He laughed, 'Between you and Mother, I doubt I'll ever get as far as haughty!'

'So long as you avoid the destruction part, I'll be happy.'

He stopped and lifted her chin, their lips brushing gently but lingering for a lifetime, 'I'll miss you, lass,' he offered as they separated.

She opened her handbag and withdrew the front door key, 'Just come back to us Reggie, that's all. Now get off before I get all maudlin. Send me a postcard when you get there.'

She tiptoed, her lips against him again, then turned and opened the door. She poked her head around it door and blew a kiss before closing it.

As always, the night seemed darker and colder once Mavis

was gone, but he knew that more delay would simply upset her, so he whistled his way back to the front door of his house.

Next morning, Mother stayed in bed. She hated goodbyes, but he also knew she'd want him to pop in. He kissed her cheek and wished her well, then squeezed her hand as he headed for the door.

Picking up his bag, he walked to the station. The switch in his mind flipped over to the job of skippering His Majesty's Trawler 'White Nab'. He turned as he entered the railway station, knowing full well how much he loved this little haven on the Yorkshire coast, but also that his ship awaited him in Hull.

Chapter Four

53° 50' 40" N, 0° 23' 60" W

Beverley, East Riding

Piers Fortesque-Smythe paused before a large pair of wooden gates, adorned with a sign reading 'Speed Limit 5 MPH'. Behind the gates stood a brick workshop building with a sloping roofed lean-to at the far end. Behind was an odd, white building which resembled a domestic house at ground-floor level, with an office or store on the upper floor. Above the upper floor window was a large sign proclaiming 'Cook, Welton, and Gemmell Ltd. Shipbuilders'.

His orders were to report to the Grovehill Shipyard in Beverley, Yorkshire. After making enquiries inside, a laughing receptionist suggested that the drafting office had made a mistake. His ship was laying in Hull, in the Alexandra dock! The shipbuilders had made the new funnel and cowl vent, but White Nab had too deep a draught for the River Hull, so they had delivered the parts to the docks for fitting. A friend of the Shipyard Manager had said they could use his crane to fit the new funnel, so long as they moved off the jetty in short order, she confided. Number One shook his head and asked if she could call him a taxi. The helpful young woman smiled and reached for a telephone, but a voice rang out, 'Elsie, I shall be setting off for Hull to see the timber merchant. I can drop the young man off, I'm leaving in five minutes. We must do what we can to help our lads in uniform!'

Just over an hour later, after a hair-raising ride in a rather battered Austin Seven, he strolled through the busy timber yard in Kingston Upon Hull. His bag across his shoulder made his arm ache, a reminder of his adventures in Norway. An enemy bullet had damaged his upper arm, and he had endured surgery and a frustrating period of convalescence and rehabilitation. Strength was returning to his arm, but they had warned him it might ache for many years. After walking to the quayside crane, he could finally see His Majesty's Trawler White Nab laid alongside a timber lighter. There was a lot of bustle as workmen passed up tools and left-over materials up to their mates on the quay. He knew they'd sustained the damage she had suffered at the hands of an E-Boat while escorting an east-coast convoy.

He lowered his bag and climbed down before walking across the small foredeck of the lighter, and stood for a moment, taking in the lines of their little ship. She was visibly longer than the first White Nab and the crew had clearly been laying about them with grey paint during the repairs. She actually looked smart! True, they might not ask her to lead a Spithead review, but she wasn't about spit, polish, pomp or tradition: she was a worker, a ship that got things done. He chuckled at how ridiculously pleased he was to see her. On the bridge-deck he could see the figure of Arthur Stainton, the mate, looking his way and using his hand as a sunshade. He waved and strode forward.

At the slope of two-inch planks which formed the brow, he paused, looking up. The Mate's beaming face looked down, then turned away, 'Alfie, nip down and help the First Officer with his dunnage please.'

To his surprise, young Alfie, nominally an apprentice but who actually had more sea-miles than did the First Officer, snapped a smart salute, 'Welcome back, sir! Here, let me take your bag; you go on up.'

At the top, four of the crew had fallen in, two per side, to form a kind of honour guard. They too saluted smartly, as did Arthur. Number One was a little taken aback. He wasn't used to such formality from this band of trawler-men, forced into naval uniform as they were. Most of the time, the only uniform kit he could guarantee would be their naval caps. In cold weather, they liked the RN issue duffel coats with their own 'ganzies' underneath. They'd told him that duffels would be no good for fishing, it was far too wet, but in dry cold they were unbeatable.

He returned their salutes and smiled at them all, 'Thank you chaps, very smart indeed, and I appreciate your effort.

It's good to be back.'

Arthur grinned. Telling the lads to fall out and get back to their jobs, he shook the First Lieutenant's hand, 'It's good to see you sir, I hope you're fully recovered now?'

'Thanks Arthur, nothing more than aches and pains now. Raring to get going again, despite the lure of the nurses!'

As Arthur laughed, a voice boomed out, 'Bugger me, Number One has survived!' The Skipper's grin went from ear to ear, 'Welcome back lad, it's grand to see you.' He held out his hand, and Number One pumped it enthusiastically.

'Good to be here Skipper, you have no idea!' The starched, antiseptic hospital ward had grated on him, but instead of discharging, they moved him to a convalescent ward for a fortnight. He'd been climbing the walls by the time they pronounced him fit for duty.

'Get your gear stowed and slip into working rig, then join me in the wheelhouse for a brew in about fifteen minutes. You too Arthur, we'll have a short briefing and get Number One up to speed.'

Number One grinned, 'Will do Skipper. I have to say I've missed Billy's brews: the hospital sweeten their tea with sugar rather than rum!'

The Skipper's eyes widened, 'Good Lord, they truly are heathens!'

With a wave, Number One walked around the Skipper's cabin, which was at deck level below the wheelhouse, and set off aft. He noticed the decks were wider than the original White Nab. Passing the wheelhouse ladders, he could see the Oerlikon guns were now mounted on the deckhouse top, abaft the funnel. He wondered whether the funnel guys would interfere with their arc of fire, but he knew that Svein Bergland, their Chief Engineer, would have considered that and implemented the best solution. Svein was well known for correcting 'mistakes' that designers or shipyards had made and his creations invariably worked. Passing the galley, he noticed a change. There was a hefty machine gun mounted at the aft end of the boat-deck. He guessed it was a 0.5 inch and hoped there would be another on the starboard side, as indeed there was. Turning the corner, the galley corridor was on the starboard side, with a storeroom to port. Inside, the short corridor ended with the galley to starboard and two sets of steps, the first to the aft cabin, the second to the engine room. He set off down to his cabin, bottom of the steps, then turn left.

His recollections of his last trip in that cabin, the return from Norway, were hazy. They had given him a good deal of morphine to keep the pain manageable until they returned to the ship. Once onboard they used less, but he had still felt distant. A round fired by a Nazi soldier had smashed his arm and the eventual surgery was lengthy. All that felt like a different world. That phase of his life, his youthful arrogance and lack of experience, was over. His performance under fire had boosted his confidence and he was back where he wanted to be.

Shaking his head, he stopped musing and changed into his working rig. He noted the cabin was slightly larger than the one in the original White Nab, which pleased him. At one time, he would have classed it as a cupboard with a bunk and seat: he now knew it was all he needed.

A few minutes later he was back in the wheelhouse, sipping Billy's tea, which, when they were not at sea, was frequently sweetened with a dash of rum. The Skipper glanced over at him, 'So, how is the Admiral, Number One?'

'He's fine, sir. Offered to recommend me for service in a destroyer, so I said I'd be damned if I'd leave this ship!'

Arthur and the Skipper looked taken aback, 'And his reaction was...?', probed the Skipper.

Number One smiled, 'I rather think he was testing me, Skipper. He looked shocked for a second, then half smiled and never mentioned it again. But I graduated from "Piers" to "Dear Boy" so I suspect he's happy with my choice!'

They all chuckled, then Number One continued, 'He also told me about your heroic rescue during the first war Skipper.' He grinned widely.

'Well, I don't know about heroic, lad. They sent us to look for survivors, so we did as we were ordered, that's all really.'

Number One looked up, 'Well, I heard nobody wanted to go searching for survivors, so yourself and a few others volunteered, based on suspecting you'd heard a noise. Anyway, father claims you pulled him into the boat, so in his mind it was you. I won't embarrass you further Skipper.'

The Skipper's eyes crinkled, 'Aye, well, it was a long time ago. Getting away from the past, we must attend to the near future lads. The workmen are clearing away their rubbish as we speak, and Svein is having a walk round and checking their work with them, which won't take long. We'll have a steady run down the Humber when he's done, it's slack water now so we'll get the ebb helping us as we go down. I'm planning to go north-about, the Caledonian canal adds miles to the trip and the weather forecast looks all right. We'll be back at Base Eight in no time. Now, I've tagged you for the middle watch, if you're rested enough?'

Feeling pleasantly surprised, Number One nodded, 'Of course, Skipper. I can do anything, unless you ask me to lie in a bed for another week!'

The Skipper flashed a smile, 'Good man. Now, I want to bring you up to speed with the job. Arthur and myself had a meeting with Captain McDonald a few days ago, and he shared some interesting information. A government scientist is setting up some sort of information exchange in the United States. It seems there it's possible the Nazis are trying to filch some example equipment from that team. They have asked us to take some extra kit over to them. McDonald thinks any spies which may know about the Tizard Mission, as he calls it, would have much less access to us. Plus, he knows he can trust us completely. Now, I'll repeat his words Number One: this is beyond top secret, so we won't even discuss it amongst ourselves in public. For clarity, we three are the only ones aboard who are in the know. As far as the crew are concerned, they landed us with a transatlantic delivery job. I know I can rely on you, but it's so important that I felt I should spell it out.'

Number One's stomach had lurched slightly at the

thought of a transatlantic voyage. Then the rational side of him simply compared it to a couple of trips to Norway, and he knew he could handle that. He nodded, 'Of course Skipper, as you say, you can rely on me. Can I ask when we leave?'

'We are collecting the equipment from Base Eight and will receive orders on arrival. I believe Captain McDonald will meet us there for an update. The top brass seem twitchy about this job for some reason.'

At 02:00, Number One was in the wheelhouse, halfway through the middle watch. They had steamed 135 nautical miles from Hull, and, assuming they maintained nine knots, were about a third of the way through their passage to Base Eight. The base was a ramshackle affair run by the slightly eccentric Captain Stevenson. He was a good man who had served as a naval officer during his career with the Royal Navy and Naval Intelligence. They had set it up in Little Loch Broom, an isolated sea loch south of Ullapool, which is in the larger Loch Broom. This isolation was by design, because they worked for the Secret Intelligence Service, as well as the Admiralty. The organisation had several training establishments in Scotland, but their main office was in London. They had decided the requisitioned trawlers should be based well away from prying eyes. The resource used to drop, collect or resupply agents in the field, needed to be secret.

They were almost due east of Coquet Island, about thirty-five miles off the coast, and the sea was calm. He thought he could see the loom of Coquet Light in the sky through binoculars, but the light itself isn't visible past nineteen miles. Looking up at the stars appearing through gaps in the cloud, he felt more at peace than he could ever remember. He knew he had found his place, beyond all doubt. The dull, nagging pain in his arm seemed to fade away as he concentrated on the minutiae of watch-keeping. He suspected that asking him to take the watch as deck officer was a test, but felt no antagonism. He was well aware the Skipper would want to be certain he was fit, mentally and physically, for his duties. On an operational trip, he would be in charge of the ship's readiness and his action station was Gunnery Officer. On a coastal passage, it made sense to keep everyone fresh by adding an extra watch-keeper, so they got as much rest as possible before crossing the Atlantic.

At 04:00 he was feeling the length of his day but handed over the wheelhouse to the Skipper with nothing out of place and all his routine tasks complete. He'd seen the satisfaction in the Skipper's eyes and he was still smiling as he lay in his bunk and his eyes drooped closed.

The Skipper breathed in the peat and seaweed smells as the mountains and sea loch combined their charms. They had slowed as they entered Little Loch Broom at 14:00hrs, water chuckling by as their prow pointed up the loch. A buzzard mewled as it quartered the flank of Cnoc Sgoraig (Scoraig Hill), off to port. Ahead, he took in the great masses of Sàil Mhòr (the great heel) and Glas Mheall Mhòr (the great grey hill). Soon, the jetty and mooring buoys of Base Eight were off to starboard and they picked up a buoy.

Arthur had the boat launched quickly and at 14:45 the Skipper was enjoying the heathery smell, crunching over some recently laid gravel toward the Nissen hut where he knew Sub Lieutenant Cooper and Captain Stevenson had their offices. He opened the door of the office and, taking in Cooper's empty desk, he knocked on the door now marked 'C.O.' and pushed it open. Captain Stevenson leaned back in the battered leather armchair he had cadged from somewhere and smiled, 'Good to see you old chap! I hope you had a good passage?'

The Skipper saluted, 'Yes indeed sir, uneventful, just the sort I like!'

Stevenson nodded, 'You're looking well Skipper, and you made good time. Now, I have to tell you that Captain McDonald won't be joining us. He was sent ahead by aircraft to liaise with our people and the Americans. Between you and I it seems the higher-ups are a bit twitchy about their reputation should anything go wrong!' He took a pull on his small cigar and exhaled the fragrant smoke with a faint smile. Shaking his head slightly, he returned to the real world, 'Regardless of their lordships, Captain McDonald asked me to bring you up to date. He has no evidence the enemy know specifically what was in the crate, merely that it was top secret and being sent on the Liverpool train. The clerk in the Air Ministry spilled his guts. A man who said he would pay off his gambling debts in return for any information which came over the clerk's desk had approached him. The Nazis made the usual arrangements, and he used their dead letter drop to let them know he was to organise the movement of a crate to Euston, and that it was top secret: not to be mentioned because the scientists didn't want to draw attention to it. He doesn't know about the mission itself but did tell the Nazis which ship the crate was to be put on, and her destination, Halifax in Canada. Hence the reason that McDonald is over there, they may have another stab if they have resources in Canada or the US.'

The Skipper rubbed his chin, 'As you once told us sir, little fragments of information can tell our enemy a great deal!'

Stevenson gave a small grimace, 'Always Skipper, always. Well, we were fortunate to stop this. They discovered the clerk because a colleague saw him acting nervously and noticed he was under a lot of strain. He reported this to their supervisor, who passed it up the line because MI5 had been sniffing around a suspected information leak. They, in turn, shared information on the committee McDonald sits on, after which MI5 asked for help. It was this chain of events which put the Nazis on his plate.'

Shaking his head, the Skipper replied, 'A good job too, sir, imagine if the Nazis had the crate!'

Stevenson tapped his pencil on the desk, 'We need every

advantage, Skipper, if we're to win this war! While we're speaking about the importance of it, I think you should keep the bulk of this from your crew. We may be able to use the dead letter drop to feed misinformation to the Nazis, but I suspect they'll know this network is burned unless SIS can turn the case officer. We know that you and your officers are trustworthy and this operation isn't in hostile territory, so I'll leave it up to you how much you say to your first officer and mate.'

The Skipper flashed a grin, 'No problem, sir. I shared the basic story with Number One, because Captain McDonald briefed Arthur and myself, so I'll let them have more, if it's necessary for them to perform their duties.

Captain Stevenson beamed his wide-smile, 'Up to you Skipper, as I say. Anyway, tomorrow is for bunkering and resupply for the longer trip. You'll have to take a trip round to Ullapool for the latter I'm afraid, some problem with delivery. The following day, the men from the ministry will drop off your cargo, which is to be stored onboard, well secured, and you are to put to sea immediately after the loading. In Halifax, you will be met by Captain McDonald, who will arrange secure storage of the spare crate, though if he's in any way worried, he may leave it onboard. The MI6 ethos is 'trust nobody' and they'll want your cargo well away from any wandering Nazis, I suspect!'

The Skipper's lips twitched into a smile, 'As Captain McDonald once said sir, the secret world can be dirty and full of deceit!'

'Sadly, Skipper, yes, I'm fairly peripheral and well

isolated, but intelligence work can take your soul if you let it. McDonald is sound though, a solid sort of officer.'

'Indeed, sir,' replied the Skipper, 'much the conclusion I reached. A decent man too, I suspect.'

Stevenson nodded, 'I think you're right Skipper. Care for a snifter before you go?'

'If you have a malt, sir, I'd be delighted!'

'Skipper, if I am breathing, then I have a malt!'

As they walked down the wooden steps set into the peat, Stevenson nodded over at White Nab, 'I trust you won't appropriate any more ships on this trip Skipper, I imagine a US Navy cruiser coming up the loch with trawling gallows welded to the bulwarks?'

The Skipper shook his head, 'Not planning anything, sir. On the other hand, if they damage my ship and risk leaving a member of my crew stranded in occupied lands, then you never know! That said, no Yorkshireman would pay the fuel bills for a ship like that, so perhaps not.'

When they had settled in his shack, Captain Stevenson poured two generous measures and raised his glass, 'To HMT White Nab and all who sail in her!'

The Skipper raised his glass and grinned. He could enjoy Stevenson's company. An hour later, he was back on White Nab and briefing his officers. Arthur went off to make sure Billy had stocked his pantry, and Number One had the lads clear some space in the aft storeroom for the crate.

As evening fell, the Skipper went to his cabin, a chartroom with a seat around the chart table, a small wardrobe, cupboard, and a bunk with chart drawers underneath. He turned on his wireless and began to read a letter from Mavis, the love of his life, but often his greatest tormentor. This, however, was one of her more affectionate letters. He felt their relationship was developing, but wartime is hard on romance. His occasional, and short, leave periods were not long enough for them to achieve the easy familiarity they craved. Often, the first two days seemed like getting to know each other again. Despite these obstacles, he had noticed their embraces were closer and parting kisses longer, so he dared to hope they were moving forward in their relationship.

After clearing the dinner plate which Billy, their cook, had brought him he lit his pipe and considered the ship and crew. He was happy with the ship: she was a good sea-boat and well-built by Cook, Welton and Gemmell in Beverley. Svein had been busy fitting the intercom system they'd salvaged from the old White Nab and had excelled himself by swapping a salvaged donkey engine for the two 0.5 Vickers machine guns. He'd fabricated the mounts himself. It had amazed the Skipper when his request for ammunition was approved. They were well armed, for a trawler, with a Lewis gun on each bridge wing, a twelve pounder quick-firing gun on a platform behind the whaleback, Oerlikon guns port and starboard on the deckhouse, and the two Vickers 0.5-inch guns on the aft end of the boat deck. Many requisitioned trawlers and drifters they had encountered bristled with armament 'borrowed' during the evacuation at Dunkerque, either stripped from damaged vessels or 'donated' by the army as they stripped vehicles for weapons which were then spiked on the beach, or, occasionally, handed over to their rescuers!

He turned his mind to the crew. Most of the lads came from Ganton Lass, the name of the original White Nab, and could be relied upon utterly. Many of the rest were Royal Naval Reserve, meaning they were professional seamen before volunteering. One man, Fred Braithwaite, was a certified watch-keeper, which was the reason he could use Number One as a traditional first officer, with gunnery as his action station. There were only two Volunteer Reserve hands with no sea time, both of whom would be tested in the Atlantic, but Arthur had said they'd settled in so far, and he was comfortable. As for his officers, he was supremely confident. Number One's issues when he first joined were a thing of the past, he was now a competent and confident officer with the respect of the crew.

He smiled to himself, yet behind his confidence he knew they faced the wide Atlantic, the old grey widow-maker. It was no idle fancy that the Plimsoll line had a 'WNA' mark — the line which showed the depth beyond which masters should not load merchant ships for Winter, North Atlantic.

Chapter Five

56° 11' 24.1" N, 12° 59' 13" W

Convoy Muster Point, North Atlantic

A rthur peered out through the Kent Clear-View
Screen; a spinning glass disc designed to throw off
water, as a squall of rain passed over. The seas were building,
but the ship was reacting superbly. She was some thirty
feet longer than the original White Nab and broader in
the beam. With the extra power of her engine and her
gracefully flared bow, she shouldered aside the green-grey
hills of water as they ploughed toward the convoy muster
point, north-west of Ireland. He'd noticed the whaleback
was more effective than on other ships he'd sailed in, much
less water entered the well of the ship, but, despite that,
he had the lads rig lifelines across the well deck to the gun
platform and whaleback. The stout wire cables allowed
them to clip on with carabiner hooks on lanyards attached

to their harnesses. He'd also had Svein weld some eyes on the deckhouse and they'd looped another cable through them as a jackstay, so there was protection all the way from the whaleback to the stern grating. He knew it was important not to ignore the power of the Atlantic, they'd had much experience of it off Iceland and in the Barents Sea, when strong and prolonged westerly winds over a long fetch could push up truly mountainous swells.

One of their RNVR lads, Danny, was already suffering with seasickness. He'd make sure Danny stayed hydrated and had asked the lads to go easy on him, but to be fair, the lad wasn't giving up and tried to do his work as best he could. Arthur knew that, most times, it would ease in a day or two and experience had taught him that, once it stopped, the lad would know he had his sea-legs, so it wouldn't come back. Many people suffered because they knew they were going to and, therefore, did. Arthur usually gave sufferers a job where they could see outside and told them to watch the horizon and move with the ship, this tended to help too.

Arthur had received a letter from Elsie, his wife, before sailing. She had been positive, but was concerned about their son, Peter, who seemed to be obsessed with joining the Armed Forces. He said that he would prefer to join the Navy, but if pressed, would join the Army. Arthur had dashed off a note to reassure her, or at least try to, pointing out he was only fourteen, so his chances of convincing a recruiting officer he was eighteen must be slim. In his own mind, he couldn't suppress the thought that in eighteen months Peter would be sixteen and perhaps more able to convince a recruiting officer by then. Shaking his head, he tried to turn thoughts back to the here and now, but his subconscious retaliated with the notion that, in the country's current state, the war could still be going on when Peter really turned eighteen!

Their wireless man, Neville Danby, or 'Sparks' to everyone onboard, popped his head out of the wireless room.

'Can I get you a brew Arthur? I'm just about to grab a sandwich as well, if you're interested?'

'Yes, to the tea, and no to the sandwich thanks, Sparks. I had a bite before coming on watch.'

Neville waved and clattered off down the bridge ladder.

Arthur did his chores: writing up the deck log, asking Len to stream the patent log, calculating their latitude and longitude, and marking their estimated position on the chart. As he finished and took the wheel back from George, their lead hand, the intercom buzzed from the flying bridge.

'Smoke fine on the starboard bow Arthur!'

Judging by his estimated position, this would be the convoy mustering, but he told the lookouts to keep their eyes skinned and try to get a positive identification. Ten minutes passed, and the buzzer sounded again.

'Looks like the convoy Arthur. There are multiple clouds of smoke and we think we caught sight of an Aldis lamp flashing too.'

'Thanks Peter, I'll call the Skipper.'

He was about to press the toggle for the Skipper's cabin, but paused when he heard sea-boots clumping up the stairs from below. Sure enough, the port-side door at the back of the wheelhouse swung open, and the Skipper appeared, duffel coat over his arm. Lurching slightly as they slammed into a larger than ordinary wave, he glanced at the chart as Arthur spoke.

'We've got multiple signs of smoke fine on the starboard bow, Skipper. A safe bet it's the convoy, I'd say.'

The Skipper nodded and glanced out of the wheelhouse windows, 'I agree Arthur, just get a bearing and approximate range from the lookouts would you, and I'll do the course to steer.'

Arthur nodded and buzzed the mess-room.

'Send Jim Pickering up, would you? We're nearing the convoy and we'll need somebody with decent morse as we close them.'

Pickering appeared quickly, wearing an oilskin smock, and grabbed a signal pad before clumping up the ladder to the flying bridge.

Arctic Flower, as the ship had been called before the Skipper took her and they renamed her HMT White Nab, had a proper monkey island atop the wheelhouse. There were strong stanchions and brass rails around it, and they could con the ship from there, with good visibility. It already had speaking tubes to wheelhouse and engine room so Svein had added a thin steel plate to the front with what the Skipper suspected was a two-piece car windscreen on top. Each side had grey-painted canvas dodgers, with a smaller dodger between the port and starboard access ladders, all that remained was to wire in the intercom unit he'd salvaged before they left the first White Nab and they had their flying bridge. Svein had wanted to see how she handled in a seaway before deciding whether to plate the sides and rear. He remembered how sensitive the original White Nab had been if there were too much top-hamper.

The convoy was no longer hull-down and there were dirty merchant ships as far as the eye could see. The grey funnel line was also in evidence and, sure enough, a signal lamp flashed. They moved White Nab one column nearer the centre of the convoy, which Arthur assumed was a way of protecting their valuable cargo. Lord knows what the crew which had taken their place thought about an escort trawler snugged down in a safer berth, thought Arthur.

They threaded through and picked up their position with minimum fuss and by nightfall, the convoy was formed up and en-route to Canada.

Arthur and the Skipper raised their mugs of tea as the Skipper slid sideways and Arthur clung to the wheel for support. The weather was filthy, with no sign of improving in the next twenty-four hours. It had been so bad that their main escort were delayed, and had only recently joined the convoy.

'I'm guessing this will keep the u-boats at bay Skipper?' Arthur grinned, his teeth visible in the dim light of the binnacle.

The Skipper sucked his teeth, 'Not sure Arthur, it would

be difficult to attack in this, but they have to surface to recharge their batteries so they could still be about. Damned ungentlemanly if you ask me!'

Arthur leaned into the wheel slightly as they sliced into another wave and eased as they crested.

Suddenly the Skipper yelled, 'Hard to Starboard Arthur!'

The tone of voice had Arthur spinning the wheel instantly. He suddenly saw what the Skipper had spotted. A merchantman was slicing across diagonally and rolling on her beam-ends. She looked to be in trouble and Arthur wondered if her cargo had shifted: she seemed to list to starboard, though it was hard to be certain in this weather. They too began to roll heavily, and the Skipper grabbed the tannoy microphone, 'All hands brace, we are currently beam on to the seas due to some silly bugger careering across our bows!'

The moon obliged them by showing through the scudding clouds; the merchantman had regained some control and was coming up, head to sea, in between the two columns. An elderly destroyer had detached from the convoy wing and came thundering up on the merchantman. The destroyer must have been doing 20 knots, and she looked more like a submarine than a surface ship, the seas were washing over her decks and white water and spray from bigger waves were nearly as high as her open bridge. Arthur thanked his stars that their ship, though around half the length of the destroyer, had a lot more of her mass underwater and much less top hamper, so she rolled less violently, and by using harnesses and jackstays, they could at least walk fore and aft on the deck in relative safety.

Arthur rang for more revolutions and resumed course, casting about for the steamer they had been following, but the intermittent moonlight was not enough to pick her out. The Skipper spotted the vessel which had been astern, now off to port, so they paralleled her course and overhauled her, eventually Arthur saw the dimmed stern light of the ship upon which they kept station, and they fell back in line and adjusted their speed. They would fine-tune their position as necessary during daylight but Arthur knew he was a fair judge of distance in anything but fog: it was almost always possible, once his eyes became fully dark adapted, to see a dim silhouette of the ship ahead against the slightly lighter sky, even on moonless nights there was often a slight difference between the tone of the sky and that of the sea.

So their roller-coaster life continued, a patchwork of bruised limbs for those rolled out of their bunks or overbalanced by exceptionally large waves, Billy's scalded arm had resulted from trying to make hot soup for the middle watch, and Fred's 'injury' after being dumped into a sitting position on top of an unyielding cleat was no longer spoken of. Fred had taken so much stick that he'd yelled out, saying the next man to mention the incident would be inspecting the bruise at close quarters.

And so life went on for the next eighteen hours.

Arthur stumped up the bridge ladders and entered the wheelhouse, with the Skipper close behind. Arthur was relieving Fred Braithwaite for the forenoon watch and the Skipper had fetched tea from the galley.

Gazing out at the green-grey surface of the sea and the washed out cornflower of the sky, it surprised Arthur how much the swell had moderated while he had slept. The convoy was now more visible than at any time since they left, and the sheer size of it struck Arthur. Also, the great distance it spread out. They were used to East Coast convoys in the narrow swept channels inshore of the British minefields, so a convoy that was wider than it was long was a real novelty. Also, they were ordered to recommence zigzagging, which was postponed during the blow, and Arthur had to get used to following the zigzag clock's signals to make pre-assigned course changes. It amazed him to see such a large group of ships all turn together like a shoal of herring.

Fred handed over but advised them to get someone to monitor the signals between one destroyer and a merchantman in the next column who periodically made too much smoke. He said the skipper of the escort was obviously a sarky bugger and the signals were hilarious. The last one had said, 'Unless grilling steak for escorts, please make less smoke. Failure to comply may cause expulsion from the convoy by means of U-Boat.'

Arthur glanced up as the Skipper called down to Billy, 'Can you manage bacon sandwiches today Billy?' A voice drifted back, and Arthur smiled.

'That's what I'm taking for the lads coming off watch Skipper. Yours will be five minutes; and yes, plenty of brown sauce on your sandwich.'

The Skipper turned to face Arthur, 'He'll go far that man, anticipating your skipper's needs, that's the ticket.' Arthur smiled back at him as Fred headed for the door.

Fred's voice floated up as he descended the wheelhouse ladder, 'I'd better look sharp and get one while they're hot. See you later chaps!'

They moved into their routine, Number One held divisions, though pared down to suit a trawler at sea. The crew who were not on watch gathered in the waist and George Sneaton, Fred Braithwaite, or Arthur would count heads before Number One did a quick inspection. He'd learned it was counter-productive to expect trawlermen to appear in immaculate uniform and shiny boots, rather he looked for reasonably tidy gear, appropriate for the work of the day and only really commented if anyone needed Billy to give him a haircut. After this, he assigned jobs from a prioritised list which he and Arthur had agreed, and ensured they were done. He rarely had cause to complain. Number One would then tour the ship and look for anything they hadn't previously spotted and, as gunnery officer, inspect all the armament and munitions. He'd go below for a 'snag list' from Svein and report to the Skipper. Aware they had inserted him into a previously successful organisation, he asked Arthur to hold divisions when appropriate so the lads recognised he was simply doing Arthur's old job as mate, but in a more military way.

Despite initial hostility, the system now worked well. In heavy weather, they'd simply assign work in the messroom, or the 'fish room' as Arthur still called it, but Number One inspected armament and munitions, then toured the ship, whatever the weather.

The pale blue sky deepened in colour as the sun climbed. Initially quite cold, the day began to warm and Arthur opened the wheelhouse door to air the place. The escorts dashed around, shepherding the convoy back into shape following the storm. The escort included another armed trawler; Arthur could see someone on the bridge-deck peering through glasses at White Nab. They'd be wondering why they were escorting a ship which was more heavily armed than their own! During heavy weather he hadn't really noticed, but with increased visibility it seemed odd not to be chasing about, herding stragglers and chasing false echoes. They had intercepted more than their share of whales and unknown wrecks during their time escorting coastal convoys off Britain's east coast. Arthur thought the merchantmen were better disciplined than coastal convoys, but he'd heard that some masters still tried to detach from convoys, and were seldom seen again. Rumour also had it that the u-boats were adopting different tactics and shipping losses, murderous as they were since the Nazis had access to ports on Europe's Atlantic coast, were rising even more.

Billy appeared with tea at 10:00 and Number One popped his head in. Billy grinned, 'You're becoming a trawlerman sir, you can smell the pot!'

'There are worse things to be than a trawlerman Billy, that's for sure!' Number One replied.

Tea-break over, they returned to their daily chores. Number One was about to drill the twelve-pounder crew and Arthur was filling in the deck log. Arthur had put Davy Roxby on the wheel and the Skipper was outside the wheelhouse door looking around through his high-power glasses.

Suddenly, Arthur felt like someone had punched him in the kidneys. A thunderous, massive explosion came from ahead. The ship ahead in their column veered away to starboard, revealing a horrific sight. An escort oiler, a tanker equipped for refuelling escort vessels at sea, was already settling and the whole forward half of the ship was burning as an enormous fireball rose into the sky, sucking up a plume of jet-black smoke as it rose. The sea was burning on both sides of the stricken ship and Arthur altered to starboard. Looking horrified, the Skipper yelled up to the lookouts on the flying bridge to watch the ships behind them and told Pickering to signal the destroyer astern and ask permission to search for survivors. The signal came back instantly, 'Negative. Reform when clear ahead.' The Skipper thumped the rail. On another day, he would have stopped regardless and faced the consequences, but the thought of their cargo and its value was in his mind.

Many of the crew were on the port rail, watching with horror. Arthur and the Skipper flinched as burning men flung themselves off into the flaming water. The fire had spread almost fully aft, and the fuel-oil floating on the sea had now ignited all the way round the ship. Men huddled as flame spurted from ports and deck hatches, fire engulfed a group desperately trying to launch a boat near the stern as another hatch or vent blew off. As the falls burnt, the bow of the boat dropped into the fiery water. Nobody was in it, and if they had been, it would have tumbled them into the flames.

The Skipper clambered up to the flying bridge to check the lookouts were alert. Arthur went down to deck level as the oiler died: she half rolled on to her port side as her stern rose toward the sky, then she slid away into the deep. As the scene of disaster receded astern, Arthur desperately scanned the still burning water with glasses to locate a survivor. There were none.

Arthur wearily climbed the ladder and leaned against the wheelhouse door, trying to take in the enormity of what had happened. He knew it was one tiny incident, among probably hundreds on that morning, but in his mind's eye he could see an army of devastated families, orphans, grieving widows, babies who would never know their father. Shaking his head: he couldn't get the image of his Peter out of his mind. He mentally straightened himself, he realised that allowing himself to think like this was a road to torment. He had to square up and move on.

He looked up at Davy Roxby, on the helm, and told him to keep station on the ship ahead. He said they'd probably ease to port and move forward in their column. The lad's face was white.

The Skipper came in, blowing his cheeks out. Glancing at Arthur, he gripped his friend's shoulder and squeezed, 'A rough old day, Arthur, about as rough as they come.'

Arthur nodded, not trusting himself to speak.

The Skipper continued, 'We'll issue a tot of rum for the lads and I'll ask yourself and Number One to quietly monitor the crew over the next day or two. I saw nerves shredded in the first war; usually it starts with things like this, and it's best to find out if we have a problem in the making. Just watch for anyone who is brooding.'

Arthur coughed, breathing deeply, 'Will do Skipper. I could use some rum myself, to be honest!'

The Skipper nodded, 'We both saw things in the first war, but this has to be the nastiest I've experienced.'

'It is that, Skipper.' Nodding, Arthur headed off to find Billy: together they'd organise the rum issue.

Arthur saw Number One on the deckhouse, leaning on an Oerlikon, and passed on the Skipper's instructions. As they spoke, a destroyer foamed across their stern, going like the clappers, and a few minutes later they heard the crump of depth charges. Arthur saw that Number One had tears of rage in his eyes as he glanced astern at their own depth charge racks, unused.

The Skipper pursed his lips as he studied his sailing

directions, the narrative instructions for passage planning and navigating in the North Atlantic. He angled his light to see it properly, wishing they'd use larger print in these publications. It was becoming difficult to concentrate because his mind repeatedly flipped over to thinking about their mission. He was trying to fathom why McDonald felt it best to send the equipment with him, rather than fly it over in an aircraft. The crate had some weight to it, but could have been carried as air freight. His only idea was that the Royal Air Force was struggling for resources, given the current onslaught against fighter command.

He turned his focus back to looking up Halifax in Nova Scotia, Canada. He'd never been there before, but the grey funnel line had used it as a base for years, so the channels would be buoyed and marked clearly. Next, he pulled out a small-scale pilot chart of the North Atlantic and cross-referenced with his sailing directions. Ice would be no problem, but they might see fog as they neared Newfoundland and eased down toward Nova Scotia.

He heard a hollow thump and immediately the intercom buzzed.

'Skipper, it's Fred, someone just got torpedoed a couple of columns off to starboard. It has to be a u-boat: floating mines are unlikely this far out.'

The Skipper grimaced, 'Thanks Fred, sound Action Stations and I'll be up.'

The Skipper thanked him and headed for the wheelhouse at speed. At the top of the wheelhouse steps, he paused with his eyes closed so he could begin dark-adapting. It would take fifteen to twenty minutes to become fully adapted, but doing this would at least stop him from bumping into anyone in the first thirty seconds. As he entered he turned to the bulky figure of Fred.

'Any developments Fred?'

'No Skipper. One explosion, then nothing. The escort trawler and a destroyer tore past immediately after it happened. They were heading astern of us, and the lookouts reckon they saw flashes. We heard nothing from here, so nothing further to report.'

The Skipper nodded, he began to make out Fred's face in the dim light from the binnacle. He'd pulled on his duffel as he came up, so decided to have a look around from the flying bridge.

As he got to the top of the ladder, a quiet voice came out of the darkness, 'Now then Skipper.'

He recognised Sid Dunsley's voice and replied in kind. He grabbed the low power glasses and swept aft, but nothing was to be seen, 'Anything new since you spoke to Fred, lads?'

'Nothing, Skipper,' Sid replied, 'We think they damaged the torpedoed ship rather than sunk her. The destroyer seemed to go further than the convoy stretches, if you get my meaning. We can't be sure though, what with darkness and the fact that we're steaming away from the scene.'

Every fibre of the Skipper's being wanted to order the ASDIC to be switched on and go chasing the u-boat, but he knew he didn't have the frequencies in use and turning on their own set might interfere with the escort's equipment.

There was also the small matter of his orders, of course, yet it still tore into him.

Forty minutes later, he stood the crew down from action stations and went below. On the chart table, he saw that he'd scribbled 'McDonald?' in his notebook. Shaking his head, he put a line through the note. He would trust his judgement that McDonald was a good man and stop second guessing his motives without the full picture at his disposal.

The convoy steamed on. Mercifully, there were no further attacks that night.

Chapter Six

44° 35' 09" N, 63° 29' 14" W

Halifax, Nova Scotia

The Skipper swung his glasses around as the convoy began to disperse. He was weary following a long night, during which some merchantmen had got 'end of passage fever' and torn off independently. He'd stayed in the wheelhouse to take responsibility for collision avoidance because the heavy rain had reduced visibility abominably.

As the weather system cleared away, the dawn had announced itself with a slight lift to the darkness. The ships of the convoy then slowly revealed themselves as though the dampness of the air had solidified into grey steel. When the sun clawed itself above the retreating clouds, he began to feel more positive, despite the fact they had lost three more ships before coming within the range of Canadian aircraft. There was still the nagging feeling he could have done more.

Looking out toward Halifax, he could see hazy, low-lying land to north and south of the bay. The town was not, as yet, distinguishable, but he could make out what he knew from his chart to be islands, but which were currently blended together by the sea-haze. Nearer to White Nab, the ships were sorting themselves out. Some were heading south for the United States, others entering Halifax. Many of the outgoing ships in their convoy had been in ballast. It was an uncomfortable fact that most of the goods flowed east, toward Britain. Canada and the United States were keeping Britain supplied, and the Atlantic convoys truly were Britain's lifeline.

He steered for the lighthouse on Chebucto Head, a curious (to his eyes) structure which resembled a wooden house with a lighthouse cupola sitting atop the roof. Wanting to be well clear of Head Rock Shoal, he stood off, before turning north-northwest into the harbour. He gave instructions for all guns to be capped and covered. While Canada was at war with Germany, he was unsure of protocol regarding entering their ports. The grey funnel line would no doubt have installed some serious anti-aircraft weaponry around their base in North America. As a result, he doubted their guns would add to the deterrent factor, even if a Nazi plane had the range to get there.

As they turned, he could see the relatively low lying coastline had a lot of fir trees and he could see why the area was called 'New Scotland'. It reminded him very much of parts of northern Britain. He got little time to enjoy the scenery, because the volume of shipping going into and out of the harbour was breathtaking. As the entrance began to narrow, they came up on McNab's Island to starboard. A frigate and a trawler were manning the boom defence, and they ordered White Nab to an anchorage nearer to McNab's Island. They secured to a buoy as three boats converged upon them. Two were from the Harbour Examination Service and checked their documents, verifying they were legitimate. As this was going on, the third boat came alongside with instructions that, once verified, they were to proceed to a wharf on the Halifax side. It was just before the Imperial Oil Wharf, and their own people would meet them there.

After the checks, they were allowed through the boom: a double row of floats with wire netting hanging below to prevent a u-boat entering the harbour. The floats resembled oil drums. They slowly edged up the harbour, passing vessels of all types and nationalities. Everywhere, cranes hauled goods onto, or off, ships moored alongside. It was truly an inspiring sight, but the Skipper's brow furrowed as he pondered the vulnerability of Britain's lifeline. The problem was the 'mid-Atlantic air gap', which was beyond the reach of shore-based aircraft. From what he'd seen in the last week or so, it would be entirely possible for u-boats to strangle this supply artery if they had the numbers.

Arthur had come up to relieve Fred, and after a few minutes, he spotted the Imperial Oil banner and picked out a group of people standing alongside the wharf before it. The wharf was about two ship-lengths long and currently empty, so he went in astern and moored port side to the wharf. The long row of sheds with a small concrete and tarmac roadway between them and the wharf-side reminded him of the fish sheds along Scarborough's harbour, now well over 2,500 nautical miles away. Arthur went down to deck level to supervise mooring, and the Skipper set about tidying the deck log and noting down their arrival time: 11:45 on Monday, the 9th of September, 1940.

Captain McDonald sat in the small office they had assigned him in H.M. Canadian Dockyard. The windows were tainted with the soot from a thousand ships' boilers, so despite the bright morning, the office had a kind of sepia quality and his desk lamp was lit. There were two other desks in the office, both were currently empty. His liaison with Royal Canadian Mounted Police Security, Chief Superintendent André Bouchard, used one. The other was to be their FBI liaison officer, who was due to arrive shortly.

McDonald had sent a message to White Nab to rest until he contacted them. He was stretching and yawning, then jumped when the telephone rang. The handset boomed, 'Horace, how the hell are you, my friend?'

It was his old friend Jack McDaid, who was a high level officer in the FBI, working in the Deputy Director's staff. Wincing at the volume, McDonald replied, 'All the better for hearing your voice Jack! To what do I owe the honour?'

'Just a snippet Horace, an 'eyes only' signal came across my desk early this morning. As you know, we are watching our man Helmut Bauer in New York, and we believe we have identified a dead letter drop which is a part of his network. Certainly someone is using it. We hope and believe that this is the only ring in the US, which is made more likely by the extensive area it seems to cover. If they had serious penetration, there would be numerous smaller networks. Anyway, whether it's Bauer, or A.N. Other, the contents are remarkable and somewhat crude. In what appears to be home-made invisible ink, the letter has a message written between the lines. I don't want to talk too much on an insecure line, so I internally briefed your FBI liaison on the contents. Eli is a good man, by the way. He's worked directly for me on two occasions and excelled. So the Deputy Director, aware of neutrality issues, asked me to back-channel the information to you as we believe it to be relevant.'

McDonald rubbed his eyes. He doubted the contents of the message would be good news, 'Well, for the umpteenth time since we met, thank you for your help, I now owe you and your boss a whole crate of scotch, I suspect!'

'Forget it Horace, just get the bastard and pass on anything you can pertaining to his network. That's thanks enough.'

'Will do Jack, speak soon.' The line went dead.

McDonald steepled his fingers. At first glance, this seemed a suspiciously lucky find, but he knew Jack would be protecting a source or his own officers, as he would himself, so he'd look at the language of the message before making a judgement.

The door creaked open and in walked a capable-looking man of middle height with a very frank and open sort of face. He had the bearing and physique of the archetypal US Marine. He looked McDonald in the eyes enquiringly, and held out his right hand in greeting, while his left showed his FBI identity badge. Eli Bernstein had the air of a man who would get things done.

'Pleasure to meet you sir, you seem to have quite the reputation with my superiors.'

McDonald smiled, 'Quite undeserved Eli, I assure you. Your Deputy Director and I served together in Military Intelligence during the last war and Jack McDaid and I worked, a few times, on cooperative operations between the wars. Oh, and please call me Horace, I dislike too much formality.'

Bernstein nodded, 'I think we'll get along: actions speak louder than rank badges in my world.' His teeth were very white and his hair was dark. His 'white wall' haircut gave the impression of grey temples but he was too young for that, early thirties was McDonald's guess.

McDonald continued, 'So I'm told you have news?'

'Yes, I do. It's not good news either, I'm afraid. There are three events of significance. First, representatives of the Tizard Mission arrived here last Friday and checked into a hotel. They were here to meet the MI5 Officer who had travelled, with a junior colleague, to escort the equipment which had shipped from Liverpool and to arrange for onward shipment. Sir Henry and other senior members remained in New York but will travel to Washington tomorrow. The second event took place at the hotel in the early hours of yesterday morning, it seems the hotel staff let in maintenance men without alerting the MI5 watchdog. Luckily, they informed the night manager of the area they were 'maintaining'. Since nobody had ordered maintenance, he alerted the MI5 Officer, who disturbed the two men. One of them hit him with something heavy judging by the egg on his forehead, but he remained conscious, and had a service revolver in his jacket. His colleague was also arriving using the elevator, so the burglars ran up the stairs. When they checked the equipment one item was missing, a kind of radio valve called a magnetron, we understand. We think they'd have taken more, but that was the only really portable item in the box and the MI5 man was getting up, waving his gun. He gave chase, but they were too far ahead of him and got away. Questions so far?'

McDonald's lips clamped shut and his fists clenched, 'None so far, Eli. It's painfully bloody clear!'

Bernstein nodded, 'So we come to the last piece of information. We are watching a US citizen of German descent who was under surveillance before the war in Europe began: Mr Helmut Bauer. We know him as a Nazi sympathiser and we believe he is involved in setting up an intelligence network here in the US. It may be the network is already in play, but we haven't confirmed yet. I'm told you're aware of this?'

'That is correct Eli, we back-channelled some related intelligence we had from the European end. One of our networks flagged a known case officer, Günter Schmidt, when he moved to the States under diplomatic cover. Jack picked it up and ran with it when he realised Schmidt apparently contacted his person of interest, Bauer. Jack mentioned you'd been watching his dead letter drop?'

'We have. An alert Special Agent saw the courier approach and, after the man left, immediately erased the chalk mark, retrieving the envelope from the waste can. Because of the need to retrieve the envelope, they lost the courier, unfortunately. We found a message, written between the lines of the cover letter, in what the egg heads say is probably home-made invisible ink. The message was, "We have stolen an item of wireless equipment from British scientists visiting the United States. Its purpose is unknown, but we believe it to be a recent and important development, given the apparent seniority of the scientists and the security around the box. We request further instructions for transporting it to the Fatherland for analysis." I have a transcript here in German and English for you.' McDonald held out his hand, his face immobile.

Bernstein continued, 'So this information confirms that a Nazi ring does indeed use the drop, and we replaced the letter earlier today, reinstating the chalk mark. We will follow Bauer to confirm where he goes, but it may not be for some time. Obviously, the other point is they are not aware of what they have stolen, that is useful and maybe encouraging.'

McDonald tapped his fist into the palm of his left hand twice, 'I agree it indicates they don't currently know what it is, but our chances of retrieving the damn thing must be nonexistent!'

Bernstein sucked his teeth, 'It seems everything depends on following Bauer. If he goes to the embassy in Washington, then we're probably sunk, but do remember, the Sicherheitsdienst may not give the information any credence.'

McDonald shook his head, 'The SD would consult a scientist, and I'm told they have people working in the same field of technology who would recognise what it is, then realise the significance of the technological advance made by us. I understand that, given this amateurish attempt at standard tradecraft, the SD might decide to ignore the message, but I'd hazard a guess that in such a harsh regime as Herr Heydrich has created, simple self-preservation would most likely mean they'll want it sent in a diplomatic bag. My superiors won't take your point as any comfort, I'm afraid, but the truth is they may have little else!'

McDonald closed his eyes for a second. The time was 23:30, and the day felt endless. Sitting with Bernstein in their office, he'd called in André Bouchard and given him a sanitised, but true, version of events. He worked on a need-to-know basis and, while he had been told to extend every courtesy to the Canadian government, the Royal Canadian Mounted Police did not need every detail. As a result, he'd revealed only that a suspected Nazi sympathiser had stolen a classified piece of British equipment from a hotel in Halifax, and they were searching for him, and his accomplice. They had descriptions from the receptionist and MI5 Officer but they were sketchy. One of them had a moustache and there was only one distinguishing mark, a sickle-shaped scar at the side of his eye. They'd also said he had dark hair. André had gone to do what he could with the border staff.

McDonald had sent a message to the dock and told the Skipper to take some rest, he would see him on the next day.

Earlier, at 18:00, Eli's phone rang, and he was told Bauer had picked up the letter. This was great news, as the FBI hadn't known the schedule for pickups. He knew that dead letter drops were very effective. The agent would drop something in a location previously agreed with his superiors. Another person, who would never know or meet the agent, would visit at pre-arranged intervals to check for a signal, often chalk marks or a certain newspaper left in a known location. In this way, there was a gap in the chain if they caught either person, so identifying the drop point and monitoring it was just about the only way to find both ends of the string. He also knew they had been extremely fortunate to find this one. It had been pure chance they were monitoring Bauer when he checked it, and they had placed it under surveillance ever since.

The FBI had followed Bauer, who had gone back to what appeared to be his own apartment above a music shop, and there he had stayed. They had a large team on him and were confident they'd know when he moved.

Their nerves jangling, Bernstein and McDonald had to wait for an hour before the phone rang again. Their man had gone to the docks and spoken to an officer on a Spanish freighter. He had gone onboard, but only stayed for five minutes. They now had a man watching the ship, which showed no sign of leaving. The team on Bauer stuck with him and he returned home for a few minutes and was now sitting in a bar in his neighbourhood, so it seemed likely that his part was over. The freighter 'Gran Madrid', registered in Vigo, was potentially of interest in the future, but they would let the message get through to keep the network active, giving the FBI a chance to roll it up once they understood its full extent.

Eli tapped his teeth with his pencil, 'We believe that plenty of goods, information, and people travel on Spanish freighters, then get passed onward to Germany. Apparently Franco turns a blind eye. Now that France has fallen, travel from Spain will presumably be simpler and faster, so it does make sense. But what to do now?'

The door swung open with a bang and Bouchard entered, slightly red in the face.

'We believe our man with the scar left on a private charter aircraft from the Municipal Airport. There are three passengers onboard and the flight plan says New York.

He gave the name Grüber.'

McDonald banged the table with his fist, 'Fantastic work André, how confident are you on this?'

Bouchard's hooded eyes lifted to stare at McDonald, 'A man with a moustache and scar next to his eye buys a ride on a chartered aircraft at short notice? Pretty damn confident!'

McDonald put his hand on Bouchard's sleeve, 'Sorry André, I'm just tired. Thank you for your help.'

As the tension dissipated, Bernstein held up a jug, 'Coffee anyone?'

'I think I need it!' replied McDonald, and Bouchard managed a smile.

As they sipped, Bernstein spoke, 'I can't help wondering why New York? Why not take it to the embassy in Washington? Only thing I can think of is there's some level of mistrust. The ambassador is long serving, so he was pre-Nazi Party. Maybe they don't trust him?'

McDonald knew very well that the Americans were unsuccessfully trying to turn the ambassador, but kept his own counsel on that, it might be above Bernstein's security clearance. He replied, 'Sounds plausible Eli, good thinking. Now, it seems clear we will have to go to New York quickly to attempt an intercept on our friend with the scar. Eli, can you get someone on him from the airport?'

Bernstein already had his phone in his hand and, murmuring into the mouthpiece, he gave them a thumbs-up after a few seconds.

Bouchard, his own phone to his ear, waved, 'I have a military transport 'plane at RCAF Dartmouth, other side of the harbour. They're on standby to get you to New York if needed.'

McDonald noted the 'you'. He knew that Bouchard's orders were to be involved only on Canadian soil, which was a shame because he was both intelligent and familiar with national security matters.

Once their calls were done, they took stock. Bernstein spoke first, 'I'm not sure pursuing the man to New York will be productive...' McDonald's telephone interrupted him.

McDonald listened for a while, nodding, then answered, 'Of course, sir. I shall do that.' He looked around the others, 'I have orders to hand a replacement item from White Nab to the Tizard team here in Halifax, then take passage to New York in White Nab to hand over the rest of the equipment to one of Sir Henry Tizard's men, and the British Security Service. They are to take it to the embassy in Washington for storage in case of need. Given what happened here, they want someone senior to supervise its delivery to New York: bloody frustrating if you ask me!'

Bernstein spoke, 'It's OK Horace, I was about to say I don't see the percentage in all of us chasing after our man when we have the New York FBI office to do that for us. Why don't I fly down to New York to act as coordinator and secure the item if it's recovered? If all goes well I can hand it back when you arrive: I can't see any security issue given the mission is about sharing technology. I'll also issue a 'watch and detain' notice on our man. It'll cover ports, airports, and border crossings, If he's still using the name

Grüber, then it may pay off. I'm less confident of success based on the description, it needs to be more specific.'

'They're all good ideas Eli, those actions will cover the gap while I'm at sea I suppose,' said McDonald.

McDonald grimaced, he always enjoyed the chase and now they at least had a slight chance of winning it. He picked up his own phone and spoke into it, 'Ah, hello Michael, it's Horace here,' there was a pause, 'Yes old chap, listen, could you send someone down and ask the senior officer of HMT White Nab to come to my office, please? He'll need an escort, he hasn't been here before. Splendid, thank you.'

Bouchard stood, saying, 'I'll get Eli over to the military airfield, then see if I can track how and when our friend came to Canada and where he stayed. It might tell us something, eh?'

McDonald's face slid into a faint smile, he was thinking he'd like to second this pair to his organisation permanently, 'Looks like we are ready. May I suggest, Eli, that as soon as we are both in place, we contact André to pass on a telephone number upon which he can contact us, or leave a message? I feel all three of us should have the same information to hand.'

Bernstein nodded as he grabbed his coat and hat, 'Okay guys, let's see if we can chase us down some Nazis!'

Bouchard grinned and followed Bernstein out of the door.

The Skipper thanked the young man who had shown him through the dock and climbed the exterior staircase to McDonald's office. Tapping on the door, he heard McDonald's voice calling him in.

It surprised him that the office was so dim and grubby in appearance. McDonald sat at a desk with a banker's lamp and telephone. He was writing in a notebook, which he closed as the Skipper entered.

'Good to see you Skipper, how was the trip?'

'An experience sir, I hadn't realised how much of a hammering these convoys are taking. I will not lie, it was damned frustrating not to be fighting back when the buggers were stalking our ships. Nevertheless, we got here in one piece, with our cargo intact.'

McDonald grimaced, 'Yes, it must have been difficult for you, and I'm afraid we have more difficulties to deal with. We must get to New York as quickly as possible in order to deliver the remaining cargo to a British organisation who will safeguard it in case it's needed.'

The Skipper frowned, 'Do you think they might need it, sir?'

McDonald shrugged his shoulders, 'I sincerely hope not, but I do need to bring you into my confidence Skipper. As you know, the Nazis attempted to grab the crate at Euston Station, which we foiled, but it appears their network must be wider than I thought, because someone may have got information on the equipment back to their organisation in Germany. Now, they don't know precisely what the equipment is, but they suspect it's important simply because of the seniority of the scientists in the party and the level of secrecy. Similarly, their attempt on the crate seemed to indicate more knowledge than they actually have, so I probably over egged their level of understanding at our meeting in Scarborough. Despite that, however, their fishing expedition culminated in them trying to steal the contents of the first crate from a hotel here in Halifax. This revealed yet another network, this time in the US. They were only partially successful, taking just one item, a kind of radio valve, but if the Nazis get that, and work out what it's for, we would lose a significant military advantage.'

The Skipper shook his head, 'So are you are implying they have it but have yet to get it out of America, sir?

McDonald nodded, 'Sorry, it's been a long day. They do, and we: myself, the Canadians, and the American FBI, are trying to intercept and recover it. Their lordships have insisted I escort the cargo to New York, which is something over five hundred miles south, but the FBI have taken over the interception attempt on the stolen item because it's on their soil.'

'I see, isn't there a danger it will simply disappear once the Nazis get it to such a large city?'

'Indeed, there is, Skipper, but we have potentially identified a couple of members of this network, one of whom was involved in the theft and probably has it with him. This is intelligence work Skipper. It's all "if, but, perhaps and maybe": deduction is the best weapon we have to hand, there's almost never certainty. It's like crossing a bloody minefield!'

The Skipper gave a sardonic smile, 'I've had enough of minefields for a lifetime and the war has only just started! Right sir, I'll slip off and get Svein to raise steam.'

McDonald stood, grabbing a haversack. 'I always have spare clothes and a wash-bag with me,' he said in response to the Skipper's quick laugh, 'I'll come with you, the chaps from the Tizard mission will soon be here to collect their replacement gadget. I told them to meet us on the quayside.'

They descended the wet steel steps carefully, then strode out toward the wharf. As they neared the ship McDonald spoke quietly, 'Is it me, Skipper or does she look more military nowadays? More, well, regular navy than before.'

The Skipper didn't hesitate, 'Not at all sir, she's home for a bunch of fishermen, plus some hangers-on. You'll find her as disorganised as ever.'

McDonald was still laughing as they hopped over on to the well-deck. The Skipper bellowed up to the wheelhouse, 'Look lively lads, the boss has turned up!'

At 04:00 they passed through the boom and headed out toward deeper waters, having handed over the replacement magnetron.

Chapter Seven

40° 54' 25" N, 67° 47' 48" W

On passage to New York

The Skipper rubbed his eyes. It was a fine day, but a lot of salt water flew in the stiff offshore breeze, even though he and McDonald were up on the flying bridge. The short chop meant waves were frequently breaking, and the wind picked up the spray. It was a 'good to be alive day' as far as the Skipper was concerned and even McDonald was enjoying the fresh air, not yet autumn, but definitely toward summer's end.

There had been a coded signal for McDonald on the previous day and the Skipper wanted to nail down their plan, 'Do you have a destination within the port Sir? We're getting ready for a boiler clean and I'm wondering if we can do it while we're there?'

McDonald looked down at his feet, 'I'm sorry Skipper,

we shall have very little certainty until I speak with our FBI contact, Special Agent Bernstein. How long is this cleaning likely to take?'

'Two days start to finish is normal sir. If it's operationally necessary to be ready, then we can manage, but the longer we leave it, the slower my top speed and the more coal I use every day.'

McDonald nodded, 'I see. I'll bear this in mind, Skipper, and if I can give you that window with enough confidence, then I will do so. As far as the destination inside the port, they assured me a launch would meet us on arrival.'

'Thank you, sir. In the meantime, we should enjoy this summer cruise to New York I suppose! It's incredible how the mood lifts when the crew know safe from attack in the next few hours. I like Canada and the United States already!' The Skipper grinned.

McDonald clapped his shoulder, 'Damn me! I cut you off when speaking about your trip over. How many ships did they lose?'

The Skipper looked down, 'Four sunk directly by u-boats, perhaps a single u-boat, and one damaged by heavy weather at the start. She made it to Halifax, but the escorts had to transfer extra pumps over to her. A hatch cover tore off, and she shipped tons of water, which pushed her down by the head and the rudder wasn't biting properly. They seemed to have regained some control when we last saw her but then she was apparently in collision with an escort and sprang some plates in her bow so she was shipping water forward of the bulkhead, at least that's what we heard from the escort commander after we docked. The worst was the escort oiler. They torpedoed her, and her crew, many of whom were burning, had to jump overboard. Trouble was, the fuel oil which had leaked from massive holes in her sides was on the surface and also burning, they simply jumped from one fire into another: Not a single survivor.'

McDonald's eyes clamped closed, 'Ye gods! What a way to die. Was this a bad convoy, do you know?'

'The Escort Commander seemed to think it par for the course. He said they are either totally uneventful, or mayhem, there's no in-between. It's got much worse since the fall of France, apparently. He said the enemy seems a lot more organised now: they are attacking in groups of u-boats and the losses are a lot higher. The bad weather probably did us a favour and disrupted the u-boats more than ourselves. It made me realise how slim and stretched this lifeline really is. I heard that Mr Churchill was concerned about the u-boat threat in the last war, so I imagine he has the same fears for the present.'

'You're probably right Skipper. They are indeed a considerable threat, but the technology our scientists have in the pipeline will hopefully nullify the damned things before long. While we're speaking about the near future, I wanted to bring you up to speed on where we are,' he paused as Billy came up the ladder with two tin mugs of tea for them, 'we are walking something of a tightrope in the United States. Mr Roosevelt is extremely keen to maintain their neutrality as things stand; though we hope that, in due course, opinion may change and he will join us in the fight against fascism. Free Poles, French, Norwegian, Dutch and Belgians are already fighting alongside Great Britain and the Commonwealth Nations, so perhaps momentum is building.'

The Skipper scratched his ear, 'Do you think our presence is an issue regarding their neutrality, sir?'

McDonald grimaced, 'I hope not. The FBI will give us cover as much as possible, and if I need you to take action, it will be in international waters.'

The Skipper pondered for a second, 'Well, I'm hoping we don't end up in a tail chase. If a target sets off on a particular heading and holds it until she is no longer visible from shore, then makes a significant course change, any ship searching along the original projected course could end up many tens of nautical miles away from the target, then lose it completely. Aircraft can help, of course, so long as they can signal the pursuing ship. So I reckon our safest option is to pen any suspect vessel in, then require her to either surrender any secret material, or risk internment. I'm not sure of the legal issues involved with that, however,' he tailed off.

McDonald nodded slowly, 'I see your point, though asking for the component directly risks tipping them off as to its importance. We could ask for the agent and everything he brought aboard, I suppose. That said, I have a lot of trust in our US liaison, Special Agent Bernstein. He's a capable man and seems to carry weight in the FBI, so, in terms of our plan of action, I have hope that he can get us ahead of the game instead of playing catch-up. Then we can resolve these issues. If not, well, we can only do our best.'

The Skipper frowned slightly. There was clearly a lot going on above his clearance level, but he trusted McDonald enough to know he would be told as much as needed to do his job and keep his ship and crew safe.

'Aye, well that's all any of us can do sir, I'm sure we'll muddle through.'

Late afternoon warmth made the air a little hazy, but the sea was calm and visibility was good enough to pick out their marks.

The Skipper had posted an extra lookout on the whaleback, a habit when entering unknown waters. They had run in roughly parallel with Long Island and had steered on the Sandy Hook light before steering west-northwest to pass north of Romer Shoal. As they neared their next turning point near West Bank light, the amount of traffic seemed to increase as the shores of Staten Island to port and Brooklyn to starboard began to pinch in toward the narrows. Staten Island seemed higher land than the Brooklyn shore, and the Skipper and Arthur were taking bearings frequently to make sure they were in the channel. Their speed over the ground was slowing as they stemmed the flow of the Hudson River.

McDonald had heard they were nearing New York and, with a wave to the Skipper, had pointed up at the flying bridge. The Skipper gave him a thumbs up and he disappeared up the ladder.

Vessels of all shapes and sizes were entering and leaving; the crew had never seen such a busy port in their lives. They slowed as a precaution and a launch headed towards them with a bone in her teeth. As they came alongside, they ordered White Nab into Gravesend Bay for inspection. When they had anchored, a workboat came alongside and a smart young coastguard official came aboard. They took him to the wheelhouse, and the Skipper shook his hand as the man told them he was a representative of the Captain of the Port, and needed to see their ship's papers and sailing orders. Once the papers were pronounced satisfactory, he went into the wireless room and sealed the wireless set, explaining that the terms of neutrality required prevention of reports of ships entering or leaving being sent by ships of combatant nations while in port. Finally, he told them they were to report to the Brooklyn Navy Yard and showed them where it was on their chart while Arthur noted the directions.

'Steam up the East River, pass under both the Brooklyn and Manhattan Bridges, then you'll see the Navy Yard on your starboard side. Go past the main part of the Navy Yard, nearly up to the Williamsburg Bridge, and on your starboard side you'll see the Kent Avenue powerhouse. It has two chimney stacks at the front and three behind. You'll see the Wallabout Basin entrance, it's more of a channel really when seen from the East River. Anyhow, enter there and moor against the long quay on your starboard side, after you pass the powerhouse.'

Arthur read it back in brief and the young man nodded before wishing them good luck and leaving.

The Skipper consulted the Admiralty Pilot and decided they could leave straight away, the flow through The Narrows would only take off a knot of speed.

As they upped anchor, the crew were all on deck, eager to see this city that few ever thought they would visit. The shore of Gravesend Bay slipped away, and they eased around toward The Narrows, with Arthur taking regular soundings. The Skipper wanted to ease as far into the Brooklyn side as he could, to avoid larger traffic.

As they entered the narrows, with Fort Lafayette slipping well astern to starboard and Fort Wadsworth on their port quarter, a cheer came from the lads on the whaleback, who were passing the glasses between themselves: the lookouts could see the Statue of Liberty and were pointing and shouting the news down to the well-deck. The Skipper smiled, thinking of that most wonderful and symbolic gift from France to the United States.

Number One was outside on the bridge deck grinning like a schoolboy with his binoculars glued to his eyes, 'Even from five miles she's a grand sight Skipper, the light green colour wasn't what I expected mind.' The Skipper smiled across at him and sent the watch keepers out to borrow Number One's glasses.

Snapping himself back to his task, the Skipper called down to Arthur to take another sounding as he asked for a slight increase in revolutions from Svein, to maintain speed over the ground. He told Svein to get Archie to relieve him in the engine room for a few minutes now and then, so he too could enjoy their first entry into New York.

As The Narrows began to widen the river to port was incredibly busy. A forest of piers on the Staten Island side looked hectic, with ships of all sizes and types arriving, leaving, unloading, or loading. The Skipper had never seen such bustle in a harbour, accompanied by the noise of steam whistles, cranes, winches and all the paraphernalia of thriving industry.

As they veered around to starboard, the Skipper realised that the piers on the Brooklyn side were every bit as busy as those of Staten Island. A ferry and two tugs angled away from a pier as they passed and he had to admire the ferry gliding at an angle across the river.

'It's not the first time that lad's done this crossing.'

Fred Braithwaite, at the wheel, grinned widely, 'It is impressive, Skipper but his ship wouldn't last long in mid-Atlantic!' Fred was a hoary old trawlerman who had come to them while they were escorting shallow-water convoys on the East Coast of Britain and had quickly proved valuable because he already possessed a watch keeper's ticket.

As the gap between the next two piers opened, they could see a smart white passenger steamer being nudged from her berth by two tugs. Only two piers south were a duo of grimy tramp steamers and an even grimier collier.

Ahead lay the large Erie Basin with seemingly quite large vessels packed in like sardines. The Skipper guessed that tug-masters would make a good living in this place.

He asked Fred to head off to port slightly. They were heading for the channel between Brooklyn and Governor's Island, the improbably named Buttermilk Channel. From their current position, the Statue of Liberty looked much grander than she had done earlier, and the lads on the whaleback were all pointing and grinning.

As they turned into the channel, buoy two to starboard, he had to ask for more revolutions twice, the current was stronger here, which was unsurprising as the channel was only around three cables in width.

Passing the northern end of Governor's Island, they had a wonderful view of Manhattan and the New York skyline; exactly as they had imagined it. The Skipper shook his head, 'Do you know what a skyscraper really is Fred?' Seeing Fred's head shaking, he continued, 'It came from square riggers. They'd rig soft footed sails called skysails from the masthead to the royal's yards. I understand the one on the mainmast was called a skyscraper.'

'Fascinating, Skipper,' replied Fred unconvincingly. The Skipper's shoulders shook with mirth as he studied his pilot book.

They passed a few more piers on the Brooklyn Waterfront, then passed into the East River. Just as the Harbour Captain's man had said, they passed the first two bridges, then the Navy Yard opened to starboard. The larger warships in particular truly impressed them. Outside the entrance to the Wallabout Basin they waited, stemming the flow, until an outbound tug had passed, then slowly made their way in. Passing the powerhouse, they moored, starboard side to, on the jetty. As they finished tidying up the moorings and smartening the ship as best they could, a large car drove up the quay, stopping near their bow line.

Arthur had just checked the springs were satisfactory when a deep voice boomed out, 'Excuse me sir, I'm hoping you have Captain McDonald onboard? I am Special Agent Eli Bernstein.'

Arthur knew better than show his hand, so he smiled back at the newcomer, 'If you wait there a moment sir, I shall check for you.'

Arthur impressed Bernstein; he knew McDonald was onboard as well as the guy on the ship did, but the crew were obviously a tight unit and didn't give things away. He respected that.

That evening they were sitting in yet another grubby dockside office, gulls screaming on the roof-ridge above them and frequent ship's sirens signalling their intentions, or a warning to other vessels. A fine drizzle coated the window panes and dancing gems of water hung from a spider's web in one corner.

While not possessing the grandeur of many New York buildings the office was close to the dock and a useful size, so everyone was happy.

Bernstein, a New York FBI Special Agent, and McDonald, sat around a table branded with coffee-cup rings in its once varnished surface.

McDonald looked down at his shoes. While not given to overt shows of emotion, he found it difficult to hide his disappointment.

Bernstein was speaking, 'So, as I say, it's pretty negative news. Bauer stayed in his apartment, then the local guys followed him to Staten Island, where he spoke to an officer on a Portuguese ship in the docks, without boarding himself. The work he does suggest he's not running the ring, it's the routine stuff any of us would hive off on a more junior member. I'm thinking of him now as a worker. He may service even more members of that ring, which could give us more of them in the fullness of time. That means he's still important, but not the playmaker. Also, we've had no sign of our dark-haired man. One of our agents set up an observation post in a warehouse and there's no hint of our target on or near the Spanish ship, so far at least. Given he could have relayed the contents of the letter himself if he was fleeing the US, we are pretty sure he doesn't plan on leaving yet. I suppose we could get a team onboard for a clandestine search, but that risks revealing our interest in the network or the letter itself. Given the cramped nature of the interior in most merchant ships, we feel that risk is too high.'

McDonald clasped his hands together, 'Eli, I follow your logic regarding the dark-haired man, let's call him 'Willow': there are a lot of dark-haired men! He must be a part of the in-country network. Also, I believe he'll go dark but not flee until he knows categorically that he is burned. I don't think he's high-ranking given he was involved in burglary, but if he convinced the US network of the importance of the equipment, then he isn't bottom of the pile either. Maybe he's even the man who deals with Günter Schmidt, but if that were true, it begs the question: why didn't he send someone else? Also, I sense he's got something about him. The way he lost the MI5 chaps was impressive.' Bernstein's eyebrows lifted and then he nodded.

Continuing, McDonald looked thoughtful, 'So the next player is the man who dropped off the envelope. Let's stick with the willow family and call him 'Osier'. He is unknown as things stand. Finally the man, Bauer, who the FBI have been watching, on the other side of the drop. Now he appears to be a minor player in this operation, even though the FBI believe he is more important in the network, so we'll call him 'Catkin'. With regard to recovering the magnetron, I believe that 'Osier' and 'Willow' are the key figures: that is, they are the most likely to be handling the magnetron. If I'm wrong and there's another dead-drop between those two then we really are in trouble.'

Bernstein finished writing the code names, rubbing his chin, 'I wonder if 'Osier' was the second man in the hotel, Horace. There's no way to prove it right now, but I suspect, or at least hope, that their network is still in its infancy, so they can't have a great deal of manpower available.'

'Well, I hope you're right, Eli. I would tend to agree, because Schmidt hasn't been in the 'States long enough to build anything too extensive. I know he's methodical and never rash. So where do we go from here? I assume you'll have surveillance on 'Catkin' to identify more of the network?'

Grimacing slightly, Bernstein replied, 'I'm up to my manpower allocation Horace. I won't be able to provide much more than light-touch monitoring. While we all acknowledge the absence of 'Willow' probably means the magnetron is not onboard, the crew sometimes go ashore and we can't tail all of them. They network could have passed it to on to Germany, but if that were true, then why the need for the secret writing?'

Tapping his teeth with his Waterman fountain pen (he would use no other type of writing instrument), McDonald looked hard at Bernstein, 'A very good deduction Eli. Look here, about manpower, how would you feel if I could help a little? I have a contact who works at the British Security Coordination here in New York, he may help us if it's just surveillance. You'd be in overall control of the operation naturally...'

There was a silence, 'I think it's a good idea, however I will need to run it by my leadership. Neutrality and all: there's a big difference between you acting as security liaison with the Tizard mission, and significant numbers of British operatives working a US case. Remember, the BSC can only pursue its interests against the Nazis on a very informal basis, and the FBI can only take action if there is a threat to US security.'

'Not at all, I'd expect that. Ask by all means. Should I sound out the BSC in the meantime? In that way, we can expedite things if your chaps are happy.'

'Sounds good Horace. I'll go to the FBI office first thing

in the morning, then come back here after I've knocked on the right doors and gone as far as I can with the management. How does that sound?'

'Perfect. I'll do the same with BSC and meet you here. See you tomorrow.'

Next morning McDonald stood on 5th Avenue and, after paying off his taxi, looked up at the International Building. He gave an involuntary gasp. The building towered upwards like some vertical road to the sky, looking like a geometric wedding cake, tiers of stone on each side of the central tower, each tier narrower than the one below, and set back from the front of the building. At each side of the entrance, two smaller buttress-like buildings jutted out like enfolding arms around a massive statue of Atlas supporting the Universe. The statue stood before the entrance doors. He couldn't help thinking the building seemed like a massive finger, pointing to heaven. It was breathtaking in every sense of that word.

He understood, for the first time, that this city was a tangible symbol of the strength and optimism of the United States. This building, and others like it, were a statement in stone which said, loudly, that a nation which opened its arms to those who wanted to be a part of it, whose character was outlined by a strong and transparent constitution, could achieve true greatness in a relatively short time. He thanked Heaven for the wisdom and vision of their founding fathers.

Instantly, his mind contrasted that wisdom and vision to the instability and terror caused by the Nazis. The people of Germany seemed to be in a terrible situation. This was, so far as he could see, the result of a profound and uncharacteristic departure of wisdom, added to a lack of any power to escape the iron fist of the Nazis. He had known many fine and decent German people and was constantly shocked both by the German population's inability to recognise that a despot ruled them, and their loss of respect for precious and fragile human life was a true abomination. To support a regime which labels people of differing ethnicity, religion or nationality under a single label, then uses propaganda to demonise them was, in his view, a corruption of democracy. Most German people he had met would, rightly, turn away from it.

As soon as that thought flashed into his mind he realised that the German people's wisdom shouldn't be criticised. Joseph Goebbels' propaganda machine, which he knew shaped the only information they received, was remorselessly effective: the German people simply had no way to know the actual truth with a cold-hearted maestro pulling at any dark thread he thought might lay beneath someone's persona, and creating fear if no thread existed.

Inside the entrance, the lobby possessed double escalators leading up to a mezzanine, behind which was a directory board and blocks of elevators. The foyer held a large reception desk. He found the British Passport Control Office, and the board directed him to the thirty-sixth floor, room 3603.

He turned the corner to see many people waiting, but quickly realised the sheer number of elevators could move many people quickly. A few minutes later, he pushed open the door of room 3603, entering what looked like the office for any busy organisation. A young woman stood and approached the counter, stopping as a voice bellowed behind her.

'Horace! Come in, dear fellow. Janet, open the hatch for Captain McDonald, please?' His old colleague Nigel Paterson waved and stood.

Janet lifted the counter-top hatch and unbolted the half door, 'If you could sign in please, sir?' She handed over a register which had removable cards so they could be filed by date. Standard issue so visitors couldn't read any previous names. Once signed in and past Janet's searching gaze, he walked over to Paterson, hand extended.

'How are you Nigel? I haven't seen you since the crew training in Scotland; now look at you in the big city!'

Paterson nodded, 'Yes, ghastly place. Scotland that is: constantly wet and foggy as I recall,' he remembered who he was speaking to, and swerved, 'Decent whisky though, so not all bad, but I'd take New York over the Cairngorms any time. I'm therefore in A1 condition, old chap! Now, you wanted a word?'

'Indeed. Can we go somewhere more private for a chat?'

Paterson grinned and pointed to a door in the far corner of the office, 'Well, let's use the riot room, it's where we hold our meetings, hence the name. I'll just check with Janet that it's free for half an hour.'

McDonald knew that half an hour in Paterson's world was a very fluid concept. He'd once stepped out for thirty minutes and came back two days later. His contact had given him a red-hot lead which had to be followed up, at least that was Nigel's version of events. McDonald smiled inwardly. He knew that in their world any information was on a 'need to know' basis, so if he didn't need to know where Nigel had been, then he simply wouldn't be told, and Nigel could dine out on the comic enhancement to his reputation.

He glanced up and Nigel gave him a raised thumb, pointing to the 'riot room' as he collected two mugs from Janet. McDonald rose and threaded his way through the desks and equipment until he entered the small meeting room.

External windows with frosted inserts let in light, and there was a pin-board and blackboard on the longest wall. The rest of the room was all long table and chairs. The first impression was of a strong smell of fresh coffee coming from a percolator jug on a corner table, from which Nigel poured two cups, 'No milk and two sugars Horace?' Seeing McDonald nod he spooned in sugar, added cream to his own cup and sat down as he stirred.

'So how can I help?'

McDonald put down his mug, 'Well now, I am currently involved in a joint operation with the FBI. I can't divulge the details but it has the most senior eyes in government upon it, if you get my drift?'

Paterson's eyebrows lifted as he understood McDonald's meaning, 'Strong smell of cigars and brandy, eh?'

'Precisely. Well, the operation is growing faster than a nettle patch and we're getting short on manpower. I was wondering if you chaps could help with some surveillance ops. Should be short term, but we need to whittle away the uninvolved and less important figures so we can target the principal players with our own men. By which I mean the FBI: we are on their property, so to speak.'

Paterson looked thoughtful, 'I'm surprised we weren't involved with this Horace. As you know, they tasked us with assisting our friends over here and Intrepid, working with Edgar Hoover and 'Wild Bill' Donovan, is making great strides, forging links between the US and Britain. This would seem to be within our purview as far as I can see.'

McDonald smiled, 'I would hand this one over in a trice Nigel, no doubt about that. As I mentioned, this is an 'eyes only' operation so I'm very restricted what I can say, however if I tell you that a successful outcome would correct a British cock-up of breathtaking proportions, then you'll see that BSC might prefer to avoid it, given your remit. In addition, if we pull off the mission, the US will still only view it as us Brits recovering our own mess, rather than any blinding success. I should also say that both C and Intrepid are aware of this operation.'

As intended he saw the acquisitive light go out in Paterson's eyes, he was ambitious and avoided poison chalices wherever possible. Paterson spoke again, 'Phew Horace, you've landed a genuine horror here! I will pass on your request to Intrepid today and get back to you as soon as he decides. Just leave me a telephone number if you would.'

'Thank you Nigel. You are a diamond.'

Paterson's forehead creased, his eyes narrow, 'Well, just be aware that we are very much in the development phase over here and are pretty stretched as things stand, so I make no promises regarding the result.'

Ten minutes later McDonald was hailing a taxi, hoping that his feeling of hopelessness would fade.

Back in their office, McDonald hung up his jacket and poured coffee with a sigh. Eli was speaking on his telephone and waved a greeting, so McDonald returned the wave and sat at his own desk. He suddenly realised he'd promised to call André Bouchard, so he looked in his notebook for the number and dialled.

'Hello André, how are things in the North?' The line crackled slightly, then Bouchard's voice boomed out.

'Ha! Things are perfect as always Horace, palm trees and fierce heat, you know?'

McDonald grinned, 'Sounds just like the highlands of Scotland, André. Now I have our contact numbers in this office, which are secure. I'll give you both Eli's and my own.'

After repeating back the numbers to McDonald, André coughed, 'I have some news for you Horace. News which I think may be important.'

McDonald's eyebrows arched, 'Good news I hope? It would make a change and I would really appreciate some at the moment! Our dark-haired man, code name codename 'Willow' by the way, seems to have evaporated.'

'Well, I'd call it a positive development rather than good news, let's see how you feel about it. You will recall the telephone message I received about the dark-haired man?'

'I do,' McDonald replied.

Bouchard continued, 'Yes, well, it turns out the information was accurate but incomplete. We had sight of the actual flight plan, and it seems they went to New York via Portland, Maine. New York said no Grüber had arrived so, given what you say, there's a very good chance he left in Portland. I called the Portland police department to ask if they can determine who got off the plane, but so far they haven't called back.'

McDonald considered for a few moments. 'Well, I agree that is positive news, André. It would be great to know that our man 'Willow' disembarked there, so we can try to pick up his scent in Portland. I seem to think Portland is itself a seaport, is that right?'

'It is, Horace, yes. Also, I think the US military have shipyards in that area somewhere. They will certainly want to know the spy's whereabouts, eh? By the way, I knew you'd be busy, so I left a request with the New York FBI office for you to call me so you can ignore that when it arrives.'

'Thank you André, you've been an enormous help, as always. I'll keep you informed and if, as I suspect, we are about to decamp to Portland, I'll let you know our contact details when we set up. I'll also call before we leave this office. Thanks again André, we'll speak soon.'

As McDonald replaced the telephone in its cradle Bernstein walked over, holding a fresh coffee.

'Was that André, Horace? Is everything OK?'

McDonald rubbed his chin, 'Yes and no Eli. We may now know where 'Willow' has gone: Portland, in Maine,' he glanced up and quickly relayed his conversation with Bouchard.

Bernstein whistled, 'Wow! At least it's a smaller area to search than New York! I'll get right on it and ask for confirmation. There is an FBI field office there, so I'll get in touch and ask for a very subtle approach to the airport and police department to see if we can place 'Willow' in Portland. If it's confirmed, we can take as many agents off the New York search as possible and return them to their normal duties. I may hive off two or three of the more experienced and able men to help on our project. Then I guess we head for Maine!'

McDonald shook his head, 'We know, with as much certainty as we ever get in our game, that three men got on a plane in Halifax. We also know that the aircraft landed in New York with one person, who is emphatically not 'Willow', so it seems to me we should go to Portland as quickly as possible. However, the fly in my particular unguent is that I have to wait until tomorrow morning to hand over the rest of the 'spare parts' which the Tizard Mission want!'

Bernstein frowned as he thought about McDonald's point, 'I guess you're right on urgency, but I think I can get us there quickly if White Nab can take us out to the South Bay some time tomorrow. That way we can coordinate more effectively this evening than if we are travelling by road or rail today, and you can do your handover tomorrow morning. Also, Jack said use the BSC guys, but off the books, OK?'

McDonald grinned, 'I think that's a perfect solution Eli. Thank you.'

As Eli headed for his phone, McDonald sat thinking. He experienced a familiar tingle of excitement, a feeling which was part experience and training, part intuition, yet so often it had turned out to be right. As he reached for his own telephone, he fervently hoped that was the case.

Chapter Eight

40° 42' 16" N, 73° 58' 09" W

Brooklyn Navy Yard, New York

McDonald was speaking to his boss, Sir Peter Hayford, 'Yes sir, I understand completely. The two men from the BSC, to help us for a month is the most important thing for me. I do appreciate your efforts and I'll leave a message with the Duty Officer as soon as I know anything. Yes, thank you, sir.'

McDonald replaced the receiver and sighed. He hoped he wasn't over-promising, but the jigsaw, if not complete, at least had some edges and all four corners in place. Plus, he felt strongly that it now felt more promising.

He had confirmed the Tizard representatives would arrive at 08:45 on the next day, and Bernstein had arranged a ride up to Portland for them both, courtesy of the US Coastguard.

He was checking his list of things to do when the door creaked open, 'Afternoon sir. All's well I hope?'

'Hello Skipper, good to see you. Yes, we're muddling along, thanks. All OK onboard I hope?'

'I won't lie sir, I'm still concerned about the boiler clean, but when we're on instant readiness all the time, it's tricky to organise. Other than that and constant complaining about shore leave, I'm grand.'

McDonald's shoulders shook as he laughed, 'I can always rely on you to bring me back to reality Skipper. Well, hopefully we can organise time for a proper run ashore at your next port of call.'

'We're moving on, sir?'

Snorting, McDonald said, 'Moving back really. We will be returning north, but only as far as Portland. Now don't tell your lads that, but do let them have a quick run ashore tonight. Keep them around the Navy Yard. I'm told there are some decent bars on the street outside the gate, so limit them to those, if you would. You can tell them the destination tomorrow, we can't afford it slipping out before we leave. What about you? Fancy a drop of something?'

The Skipper shook his head, 'I'd rather stay onboard and do my passage planning sir to be honest. I enjoy listening to the wireless over here, I've even grown quite fond of popular music; that Glen Miller chap is quite entertaining. If I had to choose though, it would still be Debussy at the top of the list. I will, however, take an Islay nightcap or two.'

'Is that an invitation Skipper?' McDonald laughed, 'Actually, if you don't mind I should like to sleep onboard tonight. I'll get more rest in that way.

'Not a problem, and I'd be delighted to entertain sir, you know where I'll be. Just bang on the wall under the wheelhouse and I'll start pouring. I should get off now and let the lads know the good news. Arthur and Svein should go with them to make sure they don't have an outbreak of morale and run amok! I suspect Number One has already found a watering hole within the Navy Yard itself, but he's not telling.'

'Ha! He's probably wise Skipper. I'll see you later.'

'Thanks, sir. Oh, one last thing, when do you expect to be leaving here?'

McDonald pursed his lips, 'They're collecting the box of remaining bits at 08:45 so we should be finished in fifteen minutes I'd say. We can cast off immediately they've loaded up. Special Agent Bernstein is coming with me and we have to rendezvous with what I assume is a fast coastguard cutter in the lower bay. We will disembark and transfer to that vessel all being well.'

'Righto sir. I'll make my plans accordingly. See you later.'

As the door closed McDonald smiled. He found the Skipper's outlook on life truly refreshing. Not a simple life by any means, but, somehow, he lived it simply, with competence, principles, and honesty.

He telephoned Nigel and asked him to tell the two seconded men they should report to Portland, Maine, in two days, and that he would telephone as soon as he had an address. If in doubt they should go to the FBI field office and ask for Special Agent in Charge Bernstein, who was based in Boston but currently detached in their area.

Rubbing his temples, he ran through his mental checklist of things he had to complete before leaving.

McDonald rubbed his eyes and eyed up his overcoat. Late afternoon had turned to evening and his desk lamp was a golden oasis of light in the now gloomy room. He was considering going for his nightcap when the door opened, and in came Bernstein.

'Eli, how are you? I was just wondering where you'd got to.' He stood and made a fresh pot of coffee as Bernstein took off his overcoat and settled in.

Bernstein took a sip, and sighed, 'That is good, I needed a boost! Yeah, I'm fine Horace and have been moderately successful squeezing resources out of my colleagues.'

McDonald laughed, 'Well done. Not a straightforward task, I'm guessing?'

'No surprises there. I played up the idea of rolling up a Nazi network, because it's an easier sell. But I was straight with Jack McDaid, who then put on some pressure by telephone.'

'Yes, he's rather good at that, as I recall!' McDonald grinned.

Bernstein continued, 'For sure he is! Anyway, we will get support from the Boston office, via the field office in Portland. The New York office will man down significantly, but the men staying on the surveillance of our suspected agents are top flight. The down-manning means we can maintain surveillance on 'Catkin', hopefully to widen our knowledge of the network. They'll also watch the dead letter drop until we can tail someone to get an address. McDaid said he'll make sure they update us on any developments regarding the dead drop. I reminded New York that Willow should remain on the watchlist. Who knows, he may be travelling here as we go north.'

McDonald looked thoughtful, 'I really appreciate the support the FBI is giving Eli: particularly yourself and Jack. In the dark still reaches of the night, I occasionally worry. You see, I was told from the beginning that identifying and closing down the supposed Nazi network is a priority so far as Jack is concerned, and while I never doubt your personal commitment to recovering the magnetron, I sometimes fear the support could dry up quickly. Oh, by the way, I have two BSC chaps heading for Portland, both will be under your command, of course.'

Bernstein pursed his lips, 'Thanks for that Horace, they'll be useful. Also, don't let the night terrors spoil your sleep. I have some news which might rid you of them in very short order, so listen to this. While I was in the FBI office earlier, I received a telephone call from my normal place of work: I manage a radio interception facility near Boston. We have a Radio Direction Finding setup and I'd asked our guys to monitor several frequencies which we believe are operated by Nazi agents. My team nearly had their ears blasted off when they picked up traffic on one of those frequencies. That means it was close, or at least relatively so. Now, we never had such a powerful signal before. They were previously either weak and from Mexico, or stronger and originated in New York. The second thing my guys noticed from the signal was the morse-code was amateurish and went on for too long, so they could get a bearing on it. Now the transmission stopped before we could get a cross bearing from another station, which would have given us a fix, but the signal strength leads them to believe that, while close, it didn't originate in Boston itself. They estimate it originated from Portland, Maine. So we have independent confirmation, within the usual significant range of uncertainty in intelligence work, that Portland is a definite place of interest. When added to our own evidence, Jack simply told me, "Get to Portland Eli," so I guess we should!'

McDonald clapped his hands together, 'This is terrific Eli, top drawer stuff indeed! I don't feel so tired now.'

'Why, thank you, sir. Anyhow, I think we're now as prepared as we can be. I gave instructions regarding accommodation and logistics. We were being given an office in the Portland FBI building, but I felt we didn't want to be seen leaving or entering that place, so we have the use of an office above a department store. It's the perfect place: an airy, private office in a location where our people's movements are unlikely to attract attention, and only two or three blocks from the harbour. The owner is a friendly, if you get my meaning.'

'Eli, I can't tell you how much you've moved us onward today, my friend. You've put the spring back in my step, I can tell you! So, what are your thoughts on our approach once we arrive?'

'Yeah, I thought we might get our heads together for half an hour tonight and rough out some ideas. You OK with that?'

'I certainly am Eli. To start, I'd approach this by addressing the things which most concern us. First, he may be skipping the country. It's probably the least likely scenario, but the worst outcome in terms of recovering the magnetron. So I'd say we should get a list of recently departed shipping to see if there are any candidates. The second concern is that he may imminently escape or pass on the magnetron. So I think we need a very discrete search for our man 'Willow'. I suppose we could start with the local police and FBI to see if the chaps with boots on the ground have any useful information, then quietly begin at the airport and look for him.'

Bernstein nodded, 'Sounds good. Pretty much what I had in mind except I hadn't thought of checking recently departed ships. I also think we should make airport and bus terminals aware of his description and the name we assume he'll travel under, too. I still believe he's here as part of the larger network, but doing that will justify resources being used in Portland, so long as there wasn't a German, Spanish or Portuguese ship which left in the last few days!'

'If there was, I'll have a job for the Skipper out in international waters!' McDonald gave a sardonic grin.

Bernstein held up his hand and winked, 'Any attacks on neutral shipping is a matter for you and your government.

I don't want to hear about it.'

McDonald nodded, 'Let's hope my flouting international law doesn't arise! Seriously though, I'm with you as regards his involvement in the network, but I've always found that a methodical elimination of alternatives increases my confidence, if manpower allows, of course. "Knowledge is power," as they say.'

'Absolutely, if that weren't the case, there would be no intelligence services, I guess. A couple of things came to my mind to add to our list. I need to contact André. We need an intercept station with a decent separation angle to get a bearing if there is future wireless traffic from the network, to get a fix, you understand. Also, I need to speak with the Harbour authorities in Portland to make sure we can berth White Nab in a convenient location once the Skipper arrives. Time is getting on tonight, so I'll address those tasks when we get there. Unless you need anything else I'm going to sleep now, I'm all in.'

'No, Eli. You've done a full shift today, and then some! You go to sleep while I brief the Skipper, by which I mean drink a glass of his fine malt whisky, before I turn in myself. Actually, I plan to sleep onboard tonight, then I'm ready to go first thing tomorrow. Oh, and leave André to me, division of labour and all that. See you here at nine in the morning.'

'Thanks Horace, see you then.'

When Bernstein left, McDonald picked up the telephone and dialled André Bouchard's number, but they diverted the call to a duty officer. He asked that Bouchard call him back as soon as possible.

McDonald clambered wearily over the bulwark on to White Nab's deck. Young Boulby was on harbour watch and recognised him from the passage south. He told Boulby that the Skipper was expecting him, and banged twice on the wall of the Skipper's cabin before heading forward, crossing the well-deck, then turning aft to climb the port side ladder to the wheelhouse. After exchanging pleasantries with Arthur, who was checking all the lads were accounted for, he went backward down the steps to the chartroom and knocked before poking his head around the corner.

The Skipper sat at his square chart table, which formed the corner of the room and had padded seats on two sides. At the same moment as the peaty odour of Islay malt whisky hit him, he spotted two generously filled tumblers which were revealed as the Skipper moved his charts.

'I can always rely on you Skipper.' McDonald shrugged off his coat, which the Skipper hung inside his wardrobe cum bonded store.

'That's right, sir. If it's cricket or whisky you're after, then I'm your man. Cheers.'

'Cheers,' laughed McDonald, 'and it's Horace when we're alone. I think you know me well enough by now to relax a little.' He knew the Skipper would remain formal in front of the crew without being told. He also knew he had not yet earned the right to call him Reggie.

'Fair enough; Horace it is. So, are you allowed to tell me how the recovery operation is progressing?'

'Frustrating is the best word to describe things, Skipper. I knew it would be tricky, but to find we've wasted time in the wrong place, well, you can imagine.'

The Skipper nodded, sipping his drink, 'Aye, it would rile me up for certain. So has it done much damage to our chances of recovering the component?'

'Hard to say, Skipper. This is the intelligence game, though. I prefer to be on the front foot and pushing at the enemy rather than playing catchup. But amid the darkness comes light. We are methodically building up a picture of the enemy's organisation and capabilities and, fortunately for us, it seems to be in its infancy. Also, I suspect this network is not yet functioning properly, otherwise there would have been more action by now. We are monitoring their communications, so far as we can, and there is no sign that they have sent the item back to Germany. There is always a great deal of uncertainty in this kind of work, but we may actually have had a bit of luck here. Thanks to our Canadian liaison with the Royal Canadian Mounted Police, who is extremely thorough and discovered that our man got off in Portland.'

The Skipper had a feeling that McDonald was less confident than he seemed, but perhaps that was just worry surfacing. McDonald was tenacious and thorough, the Skipper knew, so he would bet that McDonald would find his quarry in the end.

McDonald was speaking, 'When you get to Portland, I'd like you to stand off outside the harbour for a couple of days. I have a grave concern that our man might flee with the magnetron by ship. I know the issues of trying to track down a ship at sea, which we spoke about on the way south, but I'd like the security of knowing you could follow if he does run for it. If that were the case, I'll send a signal with instructions to apprehend him in international waters. If he's already gone, then I'll try to persuade the FBI to organise an air search for the ship and ask the Royal Navy to intercept with a destroyer. Hopefully, I can establish the likelihood of his having left quickly and then get you into harbour. I'll ask if the Coastguard or US Navy can be around so we can get it around that they are helping recover a damaged British ship.'

They chatted until their glasses were empty, then McDonald went to the aft cabin and the Skipper organised a tot of rum for the lads who had drawn the short straw for anchor watch while the others sampled the local hospitality.

McDonald dozed off to the slop and slap of wind ripples against the ship's side and a pleasant breeze through his open port-light. His last waking thoughts were about the likelihood of finding a single man in a city.

Next day, the Skipper and McDonald watched as the men from the Tizard Mission, actually a mix of diplomatic corps and MI5, formally took over the remaining equipment from the storeroom. McDonald checked off the leader of the group, then called the embassy in Washington to confirm his name and physical description, all of which had checked out. The lads had rigged a block on the mizzen boom and swung the box ashore, where the team collecting the equipment checked it over. McDonald was chatting with one of the diplomatic corps men from the embassy in Washington, 'Hopefully Sir Henry will sleep better knowing he now has insurance.'

The man looked a little disdainful, saying, 'Sir Henry has not been told about the theft Mr McDonald, and nor will he be, unless it becomes essential. The last thing the ambassador needs is for Sir Henry to be worrying about security. A lot is riding on his mission.' McDonald simply nodded.

Gulls mewled overhead and McDonald was privately delighted to see one of the MI5 contingent wiping a large deposit of bird-lime from his shoulder. When all was secure the baker's van, which they had requisitioned to transport the crate, moved forward, with one car ahead and another behind with the escorts inside. McDonald had raised a surprised eyebrow after glimpsing a service revolver inside one of the men's jacket. He assumed they were under the diplomatic umbrella to be armed on US soil.

Bernstein arrived as the Tizard group left. They dropped him off as McDonald stared after the recently departed vehicles.

'A penny for your thoughts, Horace?'

McDonald snapped out of his reverie, 'I was just thinking

that the Tizard team have a good deal more faith in our friends from MI5 than I do, Eli!'

They laughed and turned toward White Nab, 'You class this as a warship?' Bernstein asked incredulously.

Arthur snapped round instantly, 'Well sir, they were going to send HMS Warspite but we have a lot more experience in battle than she does so you're lucky.'

Laughing and winking at Arthur, McDonald pulled Berstein's sleeve and led him over the bulwark.

McDonald went aft and begged mugs of coffee from Billy, the cook, before clambering up to the flying bridge with Bernstein in tow. They stood at the aft end to stay out of the way, and McDonald could hear Svein singing in Norwegian, his voice sounding hollow as it drifted out of the dorade vent, which supplied fresh air down to the engine room for the boiler fire-boxes.

The tannoy echoed, 'Stations for leaving harbour lads. Look sharp.'

There was a bustle on deck. Arthur, with the same understated way that the Skipper had, quickly organised his men. They singled up all shore-lines, and they had rigged a slip line from the stern fairlead onboard to a bollard well forward on the dock. Arthur had positioned two large fenders at the stern and when the Skipper shouted down, they let go the bow and stern line. The skipper then went astern gently against the slip line and when this was tight, applied more power, which cause the bow to swing out. This effectively pivoted White Nab around her stern, so the bows swung to port. Number One had a few lads with roving fenders in case the breeze tried to spoil the manoeuvre, but it behaved, and when the bows were moving, the Skipper waved and Arthur released the slip line briskly to avoid fouling the propellor. By going alternately ahead and astern, the Skipper effectively turned the ship around on her centre-line and then went dead slow ahead to pass down the basin, retracing their path in.

Bernstein whistled, 'I'd like to see HMS Warspite pull that off too! Impressive.'

McDonald smiled and leaned close, 'Eli, the Skipper and his crew are unique. They've assisted me in my work, alongside doing convoy escort in the North Sea and Atlantic. Before the war they spent a lot of their time in the Arctic, which was their preferred fishing ground,' he saw Bernstein's eyebrows lift, 'I can tell you that the Skipper sacrificed his first ship to save his crew and some passengers I really needed rescuing from occupied Norway. He blew up his damaged ship after calmly bluffing his way into harbour and stealing a Kriegsmarine armed trawler. All that to prevent a more heavily armed Nazi minesweeper from following him. They then hid in a small fishing village until the search died down before slipping through the defences and calmly sailing back to Britain with his charges. He told me he would have towed his first ship back had the minesweeper not been a problem. His first officer fought ashore with some regular troops, who had the job of protecting my evacuees. I tell you, this entire crew are incredible.'

Bernstein shook his head, 'Horace, I think we're in the

THE SKIPPER GOES WEST

safest possible hands, that's amazing.'

There was a rush to stow all the fenders and lines, but quickly, the deck cleared, aside from a few lads looking regretfully at the New York skyline.

The water chuckled at the stem and McDonald started when the Skipper blew two blasts on the steam whistle to signal a turn to port. The engine vibration grew as they increased speed and headed down the East River. They reversed their route, but this time passed outside of Governor's Island to join a stream of ships heading down the Hudson for the narrows. As they slid through and headed across to Gravesend Bay to report departure, a few of the off-watch lads, who had been on deck for a last look at the Statue of Liberty, melted away and the ship clicked into her normal routine.

Bernstein asked if he could let the Skipper know where to proceed for their rendezvous, and McDonald led him down to the wheelhouse. The Skipper glanced up as they entered, 'Good morning gentlemen, how are you?'

McDonald replied, pointing his hand at Bernstein, 'Skipper, this is Special Agent Bernstein of the Federal Bureau of Investigation. He has the position of our rendezvous.

The Skipper nodded and smiled, 'Nice to meet you Mr Bernstein. I've heard good things. Where are we headed then?' He extended his hand as he spoke, and they shook.

It's a point two and three-quarter nautical miles due west of Sandy Hook Skipper. It's due north of the entrance to Belford Harbour.'

The Skipper stepped off the distance using his dividers and ran a rule up from Belford to make sure it intercepted.

'Thank you Mr Bernstein, I have it. We should be there in about forty-five minutes if that's alright? Please use my cabin if you need it, gentlemen. We're meeting a Coastguard cutter, I understand?'

Bernstein nodded, 'Something like that Skipper, and thank you for your hospitality, but I feel like I need some air. We office types don't get out much!'

The Skipper seriously doubted Bernstein's words. He looked tanned and physically fit, so the office-bound sloth wasn't quite accurate. He supposed it was all part of intelligence officer's makeup, to give nothing away.

At the rendezvous point, the Skipper stemmed the tide, waiting for a sight of their Coastguard friend. He had gone up on the flying bridge to chat with his guests after getting the lads to swing a boat out, ready to transfer their passengers.

Sweeping around with his glasses, he could see no approaching vessel. In fact, there were no vessels of any kind close to them.

'I'm wondering whether to drop the hook gentlemen. I think your lift is a little late?'

McDonald translated, 'You'd say, "your ride" Eli.'

Bernstein smiled, 'Yeah, I got that Horace. No need to anchor Skipper, thanks.'

McDonald took out a large envelope, handing it to the Skipper, 'This is a onetime pad Skipper, with instructions for use. Your first officer is already familiar, I understand he is qualified for decrypting signals, so he'll know how to use this system. Just in case you need to send us any delicate information.

The Skipper smiled and swept again with the glasses: nothing. All there was in this shallower water was the noise of water, birds, and a light aircraft passing by. Except that it wasn't. As the plane turned, the Skipper lifted his glasses and chuckled.

'Time to get into the boat Gentlemen, I'll have the lads row you over.'

McDonald looked nonplussed until he noticed the aircraft slowing and descending.

'Eli, you are a cunning devil and no mistake. You let me believe it was a ship.'

Bernstein grinned like a boy, 'Well, an intelligence officer should never make assumptions Horace, you know that. I said I'd get you there quicker than driving!'

The aircraft was a small, twin-engine Grumman G21 seaplane. It had 'US COASTGUARD' along its side and the pilot lowered it gently until a feather of white spray flew up as the vee shaped hull cut the waves. As the aircraft slowed, the engine note changed, and it settled into the water, its wing-mounted floats keeping it level once the speed had dropped off.

It took only a few minutes to get the two men and their dunnage over to the plane, then it took off in a shower of spray as the prop-wash blew white water backwards. It trailed water from the bottom of its hull for a short time, then flew off north-eastward.

With the boat stowed, the Skipper waited until Arthur was happy, then rang half-ahead, saying, 'Right lads, now we'll do it the old-fashioned way. To Portland we go!'

Chapter Nine

42° 06' 38" N, 72° 08' 32" W

En Route, New York to Portland

McDonald looked down. The scudding waves had given way to rolling green trees and fields, with an occasional dry patch of land as New England rolled below them. The thunder of the Pratt and Whitney radial engines had faded to a drone, helped by the intercom headphones they were wearing.

He was mulling their chances for the hundredth time. He knew he was trying to know the unknowable and decided that he had to stop doing so. It wasn't a productive way to pass his time. Instead, he forced himself to consider what he would do if he had come across a Nazi device, which he wanted to get home.

His first thought was that any border guard or customs officer might ask questions about a radio valve secreted in his luggage if they searched him. So he would probably buy a copy of an amateur wireless magazine, or wait for instructions rather than take the risk himself. Waiting meant hiding, he reasoned.

So how would he hide? He'd definitely keep radio silence while he had the device and he'd lie low in a place where his inactivity would be unremarkable. McDonald imagined 'Willow' sitting in a comfortable cabin in the woods with a good book. On the other hand, if they expected him to set up, or help to set up, the new network, then he might risk being more public. In which case, he'd make sure he hid the device really well.

There was also the possibility that Willow's cover involved a job in the US. Unless he had diplomatic cover, in which case he would have surely taken the magnetron to the embassy, making an illegal status more likely. As an illegal, work was essential if he wanted his false identity 'legend' to remain solid. After a moment's thought, he dismissed that one. Setting up a network needs time, money, and a good deal of moving around. They would develop a legend which enabled travel, such as a sales agent, and get funds to him via a cover company.

Recognising his thoughts were running on a little once again, he took stock: first it seemed to him most likely that 'Willow' was simply lying low in some remote or seldom visited location. Then came the radio. Radio procedures were ignored, so, following his own logic, could there be a separate radio operator? They could also be looking for someone who had a legitimate reason for frequent travel.

He felt better. Organising his thoughts had given him some reasoned ideas, which was much better than his mind flitting about.

He awoke some time later to hear a peculiar noise. One of the two crew was operating a hand-crank. The man grinned at McDonald, 'Oh for a hydraulic undercarriage!' McDonald smiled, realising that time with the Skipper, controlling his thoughts, and meeting decent ordinary people was giving him a feeling of fresh vigour. Plus, the sleep wouldn't have done him any harm.

Turning round, he saw Eli was still nodding, so he shook his knee to wake him.

'Nearly time to land Eli, I thought you'd appreciate a shake.'

'Thanks Horace, one of our local guys is meeting us, so bleary is not a great first impression.'

Glancing forward through the flat windscreen panes, McDonald could see a concrete runway ahead. He felt a buzz of excitement; the chase was back on!

The taxi dropped McDonald and Bernstein outside the department store and they went up the escalator to the top floor. Bernstein had been told that the escalator was for the convenience of customers, so they reached the office via stairs through a door marked 'Staff Only'. Reaching the top landing, a young lady came round from behind a desk which stood in front of a wall covered in awards and a company crest.

'You must be the gentlemen from Anglo-American Trading?' she asked.

Bernstein held out his hand, 'We are Ma'am. I am Mr Bernstein and very happy to meet you. We shall be here for a week or two while we sort out some import issues caused by the war in Europe. We were told there is an office we can use? This is Mr McDonald, by the way.'

After shaking McDonald's hand she turned and replied, 'Yes Mr Bernstein, your office is right through here and we left the keys in the door so you can secure your space,' putting on mock severity, she wagged a finger, 'and mind you hand them back before you leave!'

Bernstein laughed 'Yes ma'am, understood. What is your name, by the way?'

'Oh, my manners! My name is Gloria and I shall be at my desk all day on weekdays, plus Saturday until midday.'

Gloria pushed open some swing doors and opened the first door on the right. After thanking her, they entered their office. It had four desks, a pin board and blackboard on the wall, and seemed gloomy until Bernstein flipped the blinds slightly. It was indeed refreshingly light and pleasant.

McDonald glanced around, noting the fresh notepads, blotters and pencils on each desk, 'I think I might hire Gloria myself, Eli. Trying to get stationary in my organisation is akin to asking for the location of El Dorado!' He pointed to the telephones on each desk with a note by each saying 'Dial nine for external line.'

'Actually, I will definitely make her a job offer, she

thought of everything.'

Eli wagged a finger and shook his head, 'No coffee, my friend: this is serious!' He dropped his bag on the nearest desk.

McDonald laughed as Gloria entered with a steaming jug of coffee.

'Here you go, gentlemen. Refreshments. Just dial 201 and ask for more when you need it. The lavatories are at the far end of this corridor, on the right. The kitchen is the door to the right of my desk. I'm told you will be working long hours so you'll need to be self sufficient when I'm not around.'

Bernstein smiled, 'Gloria, you are perfection made human. We run on caffeine and you have given us everything we need within five minutes. I'm impressed.'

Gloria smiled and left with a wave of her hand.

McDonald's phone jangled loudly and he picked up the receiver. André Bouchard's deep voice answered. McDonald spoke with a laugh, 'Hello André, it's the travelling circus here! I need to ask a question about wireless signal interception. I know you chaps have some Y Stations in Canada and I was wondering if it would be possible for one of them to give us some time, it needs to be a station equipped with direction finding and with as near a right angle as possible from Portland, Maine.'

'OK, Horace. I'll ask at my end and get back to you as quickly as possible. Now I went through a switchboard to get you. Do you have direct lines?'

McDonald looked at the centre of the dial ring and

saw that Gloria had written the extension and direct dial numbers on it in neat handwriting. He waved to Bernstein and asked for his number, relaying to André before giving his own.

'Thanks André, I'll let you get on unless you have any news?'

'Nothing else from me Horace. I'll call as soon as I can.' McDonald put down the handset.

Another telephone rang and Bernstein picked it up, 'Hello, Mr Bernstein speaking? Yes, Gloria please just send him in.'

A few seconds later, a smartly dressed man entered.

'Good afternoon. Mr Bernstein and Mr McDonald?'

Bernstein nodded, 'Yes. I'm Bernstein.'

'Good afternoon, sir. I'm Special Agent O'Toole from the Portland field office. I'm afraid we may have something of a problem.'

Fifteen minutes later, they passed through a police cordon and stood on a wharf on Portland's waterfront. Hidden behind a pile of crates was the crumpled figure of a man laying in a pool of dark blood. Someone had sliced his throat right across and his jacket was open.

Standing to one side was a man McDonald thought he recognised. The man looked up and met his eyes.

'What the hell are we dealing with here? The BSC sent us for a simple locate and capture exercise and now my colleague is dead.'

McDonald straightened, 'You can take the accusation out of your voice. We had no more thought of murder than you did! So what happened and who are you?'

The man took two deep breaths, 'I am Peter Simmons, and this is, or rather was, Gordon Woodcock. Mr Paterson told us to come here and do some digging around for a dark-haired man with a scar next to his eye, scoop him up, and then get back to the New York office sharpish.'

McDonald clenched his fists, 'Was there any mention of waiting for me or Mr Bernstein before wading in?'

Simmons was gulping repeatedly, clearly distressed, 'Only that you would be arriving shortly after us, but he was sure we could locate the man and have this thing nailed before you got here! For God's sake, we were just asking around!'

McDonald's eyes were like ice, 'No Simmons, thanks to Mr Paterson, you were flagging up to a Nazi agent that we are on to him! I'll have Nigel's bloody head for this.'

McDonald forced the emotion down, 'Were you chaps close?' he nodded down at Woodcock's body.

'Friends for years sir, so, yes.'

McDonald touched his shoulder, 'Get back to the FBI office and take an hour for yourself. It seems to me that you and your mate were blameless in this and for that I am deeply sorry. Nevertheless, we must try to recover the situation so you could help us capture whoever did this when you feel up to it. Alright?'

Simmons nodded, 'Thank you, sir. I appreciate that.' He

then shuffled off with his head down.

O'Toole coughed, 'There's a guy over there who may have seen the murderer. He's a well known drunk, but he's as sober as he ever is this afternoon.' He nodded toward an unkempt man leaning against a bollard a few yards down the wharf.

McDonald grimaced, 'Your turn Eli?'

Bernstein nodded and led the way over to the witness.

'Good afternoon sir, may I take your name, please?

'Bernie. Bernie Tasker; and you?'

Bernstein held up his badge, 'Special Agent in Charge Bernstein, Mr Tasker. Federal Bureau of Investigation. Maybe you could talk me through what you saw today?'

Tasker nodded, 'Not much to say, really. I was walking down to the end of the wharf to cast a line,' he waved at a fishing rod leaning against the bollard, 'and I see a big, blonde-haired guy with blood on his shirt. I ask if he's OK, and he told me he'd slipped with a filleting knife. He was clutching his hand to his chest. I asked if he needed help and he said no. He told me he was just about to go to the doc to get it stitched up. A lot of the local fishermen go to the doc. He can fix that sort of damage up real good for a quarter, using whisky and some twine, so I thought no more about it. I came over to check his fishing gear was safe,' his eyes looked sideways and Bernstein suppressed a cough, 'but there wasn't no gear. I walked around the other side and there was the dead guy, so I asked Billy, in the coffee shop, to call the cops.' He was pointing to what looked like an ice-cream or pretzel stand. Tasker continued, 'Billy didn't see nothing, he was serving a customer.'

Bernstein continued with his note-taking and when finished he clarified a couple of points, asked where he could find the doc, then took Tasker's address, and thanked him. He waved at a police officer and asked him to take a formal statement from Mr Tasker.

Questioning the man at the 'Coffee Shop' corroborated Tasker's story. He said the police had already taken his statement. O'Toole knew the old guy called 'the doc' and went off to speak to him as another police car turned up, the officers got out to control a gathering crowd.

McDonald and Bernstein strolled off down the wharf.

'So what gives Horace? And who the hell is Nigel?'

McDonald grimaced, 'He's the soon to be ex intelligence officer at the BSC who was clearly miffed at my filching two of his men. He's a politician, self publicist and ladder-climber and I'll be taking steps to have him disciplined as soon as I get to a phone.'

Bernstein nodded, 'Yeah, I kinda got a sniff of his character from your exchange with Simmons. What about Tasker's statement?'

'Well, it seems fair enough. Obviously I was shocked to hear it was a big blonde haired chap and not our 'Willow'. Also, blondie, let's call him Sallow, seems to be a local given he knows the back-street quack some people seem to prefer. Other than a foiled case of fishing tackle theft, that's all I noticed.'

Bernstein sucked his teeth, 'Yeah, that was what I took away too. Damn it! Just as I get the labour, we lose a guy and double the number of suspects in one afternoon. I mean no disrespect to your dead colleague by that, but this bunch of Nazi creeps are getting under my skin.'

McDonald stared out at a quaint little steamer. A narrow, streamlined hull with an upper deck full of passengers. How can people travel home from their work, or take Granny for a picnic, while in the same place someone else cuts throats? What degrees of deprivation, hatred and fanaticism turns off basic human instincts and decency? He shook his head and turned to Bernstein.

'Me too, Eli. But we must go on, we must succeed. We must make sure that extreme fanatics don't carry the day. Even if we weren't at war, I'd fight against this behaviour on principle.'

Bernstein looked at the floor, 'Horace, I've heard such terrible things from Jewish refugees. Singled out, hated, reviled and mistreated. Not because they are opposing Hitler, not because they have a different worldview to most German people; no, it's simply because they are Jewish and those who are interested only in power for its own sake need an enemy. Let's just hope he has more enemies than he can cope with now.'

McDonald clapped him on the back, 'Come on, Eli, let's get back to the office and put our thinking caps on. I'm pretty bloody certain that this time, evil will not overcome decency in the long run. It's just a question of how many lives we must waste before that happens...

The sun rose from the grey mistiness of dawn. The lookouts on the flying bridge relished the warmth, flapping their arms against their duffel coats.

In the wheelhouse, Arthur was handing over the watch to the Skipper. They spoke quietly at the chart table.

'What amazed me were the lights at night. No blackout at all! I tell you Reggie, it's amazing how quickly you get used to full darkness at home. Even at sea, we have lights on in peacetime!'

'It's true, Arthur. Captain McDonald mentioned the crowds when he was ashore. I'm not sure I'd like that: they can only jostle me a certain number of times before I feel like jostling back!'

Arthur gave a belly laugh, 'You're such a grumpy bugger sometimes, Reggie. I swear I don't know where you get it from!'

'Well, we both know that T'Owd Skipper was a pretty level-headed chap, so I'm leaning toward the woman with the rolling pin and strict sense of right and wrong!'

'By, you'd get some rolling pin all right, if Mother heard that!'

'I would that, Arthur, most definitely. Speaking of the folks at home, I have now got a telephone number for the mail office at the base in Halifax. When we eventually get in at Portland, I'll ring them and ask if they can get mail to us. I think it'll be good for morale.'

'Wouldn't hurt Skipper. I think the lads are all right, but there's a certain amount of moaning that they didn't see the sights in New York. Understandable, I suppose, but I told them it's a small sacrifice compared to being in the army in France before Dunkerque or in Norway. But, yes, letters from home would be a grand idea.'

The Skipper nodded, he was stooping over his chart and fiddling with his protractor and parallel rules. He turned to the helmsman, 'We'll come up to 347° George, just to allow for the set and drift from the tide.'

George, their lead hand, nodded, 'No bother Skipper,' and gently pushed the top spoke of the wheel over, while watching the compass in the binnacle.

'347° Skipper.'

'Thanks George.'

As Arthur went to see Billy for some breakfast, the Skipper took a turn around the bridge-deck and went up to see the lookouts on the flying bridge. He chatted for a few minutes, then caught a whiff of bacon and headed back to the wheelhouse at speed. In fair weather, he and Arthur normally let the new watch eat before they got their meal, and today he was peckish, so maple flavoured bacon would really hit the spot. Billy said they ought to give up fishing when the war ended, and import the stuff into Britain from North America. As always, Billy and Svein seemed able to barter or beg something decent whenever they entered a new port, whether it be food or spare parts.

Once they had eaten, Arthur went to help Number One with his morning divisions before grabbing a nap. They settled into their seagoing routine with ease and the Skipper knew that being in neutral waters was a big factor in the crew's relaxed mood. Yet he knew his lads would keep their professionalism even under threat, they would just be a lot more serious than they were today.

He took another walk up to the flying bridge with his binoculars hanging round his neck. He'd seen Number One go up after divisions and wanted to chat with him.

'Hello Number One, lovely day.'

His first officer turned and smiled, 'It certainly is Skipper. All the better for visiting Maine, I have to say.'

'Really? What's the attraction with Maine in particular?'

The younger officer coloured slightly, 'Ah, yes, it's just that a girl I know was invited over here to join the Portland Maine Symphony. She performs with the orchestra, but she also runs a music school from her own home, where she teaches violin.'

'So you're never short of a fiddle then, sir,' opined Sid Dunsley, one of the deckhands.

Number One turned, 'Mr Dunsley, at what point did you develop your love of scrubbing decks? I only ask because I can see no other reason for making such a coarse comment about my friend?'

Sid reddened, 'Er, yes sir, I mean no, sir. Sorry, sir.'

Number One's eyes twinkled, 'I should think so too. Your apology has reduced your punishment to fetching me a strong cup of black coffee with two sugars. Off you go.'

Dunsley sprinted to the ladder calling, 'One for you Skipper?'

The Skipper stifled his mirth and looked over the railing, 'No thanks Sid, you've got enough on, I suspect.'

Number One was grinning as he swept his binoculars

around a slow arc. The rest of the lookouts smirked and did the same.

The Skipper looked at Lieutenant Piers Fortesque-Smythe, son of Admiral Sir Nigel Fortesque-Smythe, and shook his head. The transformation of this young man in the past year had been spectacular. His leadership skills and confidence had blossomed since he joined the crew and the Skipper was happy with that.

Leaning in, he muttered, 'Well handled Number One.'

Two hours later, Arthur reappeared, looking a little bleary and clutching his usual mug of tea. The Skipper had developed a taste for coffee in the morning but was told that too much caffeine in a day could be a bad thing, so he exercised a certain amount of self discipline.

'Now then Skipper. How are we doing?'

'Pretty well, the cross-tide is slowing now so we'll make a better speed over the ground shortly.'

'That's good; how are you getting on Number One?'

'Not too bad, Arthur, not bad at all.'

Arthur nodded as the Skipper spoke, 'Fair to middling, as my good lady says.'

The Skipper beckoned them over to the back of the flying bridge, 'I wanted a quiet word with you both, while we have time. Now, Captain McDonald briefed me yesterday evening, and it seems the bird they're trying to catch is, or at least is likely to be, in Portland. The suspected spy has taken some radio component, which is a British invention, and can't be allowed to get to Germany. It would cost us an important advantage. Now, before you ask, I don't know what that advantage is, but I do know that Captain McDonald is worried. The Americans are helping as much as their neutrality legislation allows, but it's a complicated situation. Anyway, our job for the first few days will be to discretely patrol outside Portland and await any instructions to follow a suspect vessel, then stop it in international waters so we don't get the United States into hot water. We'll tell the lads it's an exercise, at least to begin with. All clear?'

Arthur and Number One nodded, each looking thoughtful.

The Skipper continued, 'I will not lie chaps, after the trip here I'd rather be out hunting u-boats, but this is the job we were given, so we'll do it to the best of our ability. Agreed?'

'Yes!' said the other two in perfect unison.

The late afternoon sun lanced through the office windows as the ever diligent Gloria brought in a jug of coffee, 'I'll be off now gentlemen. Anything you need before I leave?'

McDonald smiled, 'No Gloria, thank you so much for all your help today. You've made us very welcome and we're extremely comfortable.'

'No problem, Mr McDonald, it's all part of the service.' With a backward wave, she was gone.

McDonald picked up the telephone and dialled Nigel Paterson. He gave him both barrels, clarified that his unprofessional behaviour was unacceptable, and that he would hear more about it. After taking a minute to calm down, he spoke.

'Eli, something occurs to me, I came up with it while thinking things through on the plane, and it won't go away.'

Bernstein put down his notebook and steepled his fingers, 'OK, you have my attention Mr Holmes.'

Laughing, McDonald looked up, 'Oh if only I could look up a train schedule, analyse a speck on a coat, then walk straight to 'Willow's' hideout! No, this is much less brilliant. If I were setting up a network over here, I wouldn't want to leave a trail of mayhem behind me to flag up my activities. The same goes for escaping the scene of the robbery and getting the magnetron out of the country. You know as well as I that, in our business, we need to blend in. Disappear into the crowd, if you will. Now, it occurred to me that the slow morse, clumsy secret writing and, most definitely, murdering someone who makes an enquiry, all indicate an amateur while 'Willow's' actions have been professional. I asked myself what I would do if I were in Willow's shoes and, frankly, I'd be in a rented backwoods cabin catching up on a bit of reading until I received orders! With me so far?'

Bernstein nodded, 'Yeah, sure.'

'Good. So I began to wonder if he has a separate radio operator, or assistant, who is much less able than he is. We both know that today's murder may simply be bad luck, such as encountering a criminal with a knife, or being attacked because of mistaken identity, many things really.'

'OK, you're making sense so far,' Bernstein leaned forward.

'But what if 'Sallow' is a low grader helping 'Willow' and perhaps even trying to carve a niche for himself in the network? This removes the conundrum of Willow acting like a professional one minute, and an idiot the next. If we can refocus on Sallow, and get local law enforcement to keep us clued in while they are hunting for him we ease or own manpower problem, but may also get a lead to Willow's location. What do you think?'

Bernstein considered for a moment, 'I'm uncertain, as yet, about the link with Willow, but the timing of the murder is certainly suspect. I suppose there is no downside here, If you're right, we are in clover, and if not, then our own efforts aren't compromised. How much do we need to tell the Police Department would you say?'

McDonald shrugged, 'I'd say the people on the ground, the detectives and police officers, would benefit from knowing that their quarry might pose a threat to them and they need to be prepared for a fast and violent response. We owe them that, but I don't think they need inducting fully into our mission. What's your view?'

'The same I think. I'll say that the person involved could be linked with the mob, so they should approach with caution and never engage him alone.'

McDonald thought for a moment, 'Yes, that should cover it. We must keep a low profile. The organised crime link gives us a smokescreen if needed.'

Bernstein nodded and reached for his telephone.

Chapter Ten

43° 39' 29" N, 70° 15' 30" W

Portland, Maine

Next morning, McDonald and Bernstein were in the office early and had tasked Peter Simmons, the BSC man, with searching for recently departed ships with the Captain of the Port. They were hoping to see no Spanish or Portuguese ships on the list.

McDonald's telephone jangled and Bouchard's voice boomed out, 'Good morning Horace, how are you?'

'Losing gracefully dear boy, that's the best I can offer!' Bouchard's laugh was deafening in McDonald's ear.

'Well, I'm going to add to your woes, unfortunately. All the Y Stations are at full capacity, feeding data to Station X. I assume they read you into their work? I am not briefed, so please avoid detail, but I was told to tell you that, so you'd realise how important the work is.'

'I am André, and thank you. I should really have considered that. Well, not to worry. There are other ways to skin a cat. Is everything OK at your end?'

'I'm at a standstill now, Horace. Nothing came from buses and trams, sadly. To be honest, I'm thinking we've already got all the useful information we'll get here in Halifax, but let me know if there's anything else I can do, eh?'

'I will André, thanks again for your help.'

Bernstein had made a pot of coffee while McDonald was busy. McDonald took a sip and grimaced toward Bernstein.

'It seems we can't use the Canadian intercept stations. They are busy on a top-secret job, which takes all of their capacity. He also got nothing from buses or trams, so we seem to have no trail leading to Willow's network in Halifax. I suppose that's good news, really.'

Bernstein nodded, 'Yeah, I guess so. Listen, we need a fix next time they transmit, so I'll ask my guys to send the mobile direction finding unit up here. Also, I have an idea that we had an older set with a loop aerial kicking around, which your guys on White Nab might find a use for. That way we'll have a more accurate fix, though the loop aerial needs a longer transmission to get a bearing because it's manual rotation, but, hey, our man seems to like long transmissions! I'll ask them to check it works and send it up. It's only gathering dust where it is.'

'That sounds useful, Eli, thank you.'

They were just sipping their coffee, and in Bernstein's case, eating a doughnut for breakfast, which appalled

McDonald, when the telephone on McDonald's desk rang once again.

'Hello Horace, how are you?'

'Oh hello sir, I'm fine, thank you.'

'Excellent, good to hear. It's just a couple of catchup points, really. First thing is Paterson. I had a call from Stephenson a little earlier and he tells me he's returning Paterson to Britain. He tells me that your intervention was not the cause of his decision. Paterson reported your conversation in terms which didn't reflect well on you, I'm afraid, but which immediately proved to be tosh when Stephenson spoke to the FBI and his surviving SIS officer. Stephenson already had reservations, he recognised Paterson as a loner and a career climber by nature. What he wants are intelligence officers, not yes-men! Anyway, one of the office staff had earlier reported an outburst by Paterson, and Stephenson had already acted by the time Paterson misreported your conversation. I tell you this because, when he gets back to England, I intend offering Paterson either a return to his regiment, or the dullest job in the hottest country I can find. If he chooses the latter, you may encounter him again, sadly.'

'I won't be kept awake by that information, sir, but thank you for telling me. It was very considerate.'

'Not at all dear boy, now, how are things going over there?'

McDonald sighed, 'Well, the manpower situation is in hand at the moment, sir. The local police are doing all the hard yards with the murder investigation, and Special Agent Bernstein is liaising, in fact, he's going over for a briefing shortly, so we'll know more later. That's the highlight at the moment I fear. For the rest, we've taken steps to identify any ships from Nazi-leaning nations, you know which ones I refer to. If any left since the theft took place, then I might need the Navy to help with an intercept. White Nab is faster than many freighters but mightn't overhaul her quickly enough to be sure of stopping her before she enters port. Beyond that, I have a theory, only intuition at the moment, that we are dealing with two men, one of whom is an absolute amateur and the other a professional. The person who killed poor Woodcock has blonde hair, so we know that either the murder is unrelated, or there are two agents in play. We've assigned the codename Sallow to him, by the way. I suspect that our man, the one who escaped with the magnetron, is using another chap from their infant network to do the work so he can lie low. We're also doing a formal briefing for the special agents from the Portland FBI office this morning so that we can begin to search for 'Willow' with the right information and in the right area this time!'

'Two things Horace, I always trust the instincts of a field agent or case officer; and you have been both in your time. The second is that dead ends happen on every investigation, don't take it to heart. Now, I will not lie, C has been getting twitchy, but it looks like the incomplete information led you to a perfectly reasonable conclusion and you are recovering from the setback both quickly and professionally. Know this Horace, as I said before you left, you have my absolute support and confidence. There is no political element to this. I've already signalled Stephenson and explained that, whatever Paterson may have said, the BSC are not taking over just because you are all on US soil. Stephenson is busy developing his U.S. operations, so he's happy enough to leave it with us. So dear boy, deep breaths and carry on is the only other advice I have!'

McDonald laughed, 'You're an expert at the pep talk, sir, but I do appreciate your support. If there's nothing else, I'd better get off.'

'Nothing else Horace. Good luck dear boy.'

'Thank you, sir. Goodbye.'

Bernstein smiled, 'That seemed to go well?'

'Not bad, Eli. They have repatriated Paterson because of previous misdemeanours and my boss is behind us. The bad part was that the top man in our organisation is getting twitchy, but overall it was positive.'

'OK my friend, I'll go speak with Portland Police Department and see where we stand with the murder investigation. We'll have the six FBI guys here at ten fifteen for a briefing, so I'll return at ten or before.'

'Righto Eli, I'll see you then. I shall make some notes for the briefing, so we miss nothing.'

At ten thirty, they opened the windows and began their briefing. McDonald and Bernstein had agreed the agenda items as he arrived, just before the meeting started. The list was more complete for the FBI than for the police. Bernstein had said the police had all relevant facts, but he had played the national security card on much of the background, whereas the FBI were getting full disclosure.

Bernstein began the briefing by outlining their objectives. To recover an item stolen by the emerging network of agents, which would remove a significant advantage Britain currently held over the Nazis, and to identify, and eventually arrest, the members of the network. He explained McDonald was present only for recovery of the stolen item, but that he had volunteered help, which had been of great help to the FBI. Keeping things upbeat, he said they were getting a toe-hold on the first step to unmasking a Nazi network. He repeated that recovery of the item was not a matter for US intelligence, whereas the network itself was, but explained that the two things were so intertwined at the moment that they were working hand in hand in the interests of US national security.

With that point out of the way, Bernstein gave a sketch of events to date and described 'Willow' and their idea of starting an extremely low-key enquiry, starting at the airport. One junior agent was scribbling in a notebook as Bernstein described their current working theories, to make sure they had the codenames correctly. Before winding up the briefing, he mentioned McDonald had a British vessel with anti-submarine capability standing by in case the

Nazis tried to get their man out using a u-boat, He stressed the ship could not attack a u-boat in US waters, but could at least detect it until the US Navy or Coastguard could send a suitable ship. Sullivan, the senior local FBI man, stayed behind after the briefing closed to discuss some internal organisational matters, then they were alone.

McDonald cleaned off the blackboard where they had put up codenames and turned to Bernstein, 'So how did the police briefing go, Eli?'

Bernstein poured two coffees and turned, 'Yeah, sorry I was so late getting back. They had only just found the local quack, and were interviewing him, so I sat in. He swears nobody visited him with a cut to their hand, and I believe him. It confirms the murderer made up the 'cut hand' story, as if we didn't know! I made the point to the police lieutenant that the suspect knew about the doc, meaning he was most likely a local, just to be sure that's lodged in their mind as they investigate. They're pulling in the drunk and asking him to read through their mugshot albums for our man, Sallow. Now, I think we should go grab a bite, there's a food stall opposite, so I'll go fetch something, then we can go back to see if we can help?'

'I agree,' McDonald nodded, 'I'm getting peckish myself. I'll check in with André before we go out, though.'

There was a knock at the door, and Simmons walked in, 'Good news sir, no suspect ships have left in the past week but a Spanish freighter arrived yesterday and will be here for a few days waiting for some cargo to be delivered. Sounds promising, I think?' He put a scribbled note of the ship's name, port of registration, and the wharf where she moored. McDonald glanced at it, S.S. Posadilla, registered in Cadiz. The port interested him because evidence had come to light that u-boats were being serviced in Cadiz.

McDonald stood, smiling broadly, 'Well done Simmons, excellent work.'

'Thank you, sir. I wondered about the airport. One of the FBI lads said that they keep passenger lists, so I wondered about a trawl through?'

Bernstein called over, 'I've got the FBI applying for a warrant on that gents, but I'd appreciate your help when it comes through Mr Simmons. You'll need to be partnered with a Special Agent who will be exercising the warrant under U.S. law. I'll find out who he is and you can pair up with him after lunch if you like?'

'Suits me sir, thank you. I'll nip down to the FBI office after a grab a bite.'

McDonald coughed, 'By the way, the investigation into Woodcock's death is in full swing now Peter. It's still in the early stages, but they have proof the murderer is local and have the witness going through their mugshot archive as we speak. They're also making door-to-door enquiries to identify the direction in which the man left. As I say, early days, but at least it's not a brick wall.'

Simmons offered a wan smile and thanked him before leaving.

Bernstein returned with the food, a hotdog which looked very unappetising to McDonald, but which tasted superb. When they finished McDonald poured coffee and sat down opposite Bernstein's desk.

'So, what do we do about the Spanish freighter, Eli? I'd say we need to get a watch on it as quickly as we can.'

Bernstein nodded, dabbing mustard from his mouth, 'Absolutely. I was wondering what you thought about bringing White Nab into harbour but well away from the wharf where the Spaniard will is now berthed. We could ask your Skipper to have random members of the crew swing by every hour or two and report anything they see. When I set up a formal observation position they might man it?'

'I can't see why not Eli. I'll give them a good briefing on staying unobtrusive, also I think our cover story about them patrolling in Casco Bay is wafer thin, given the number of US Navy ships in the area, so, yes, good idea.'

'I'll call the field office and ask if they have contact with the Captain of the Port. We'll need his help to berth White Nab where we want her.'

McDonald clicked his fingers, 'I'll give André a call to bring him up to date.'

Dialling Bouchard's number, he smiled on hearing the Mounty's sonorous voice answer.

'André, my dear chap, how are you?'

McDonald brought Bouchard up to speed and gave him their current working theories. When he mentioned Sallow, André interrupted, 'Big man with blonde hair. Wait for a few seconds please, Horace.'

After almost a minute he returned to the telephone, 'I have it, Horace. Now this is tenuous in the extreme but worth mentioning. I have an RCMP report from a Miss

Martin, made on the night of the burglary. She was putting out trash in the alley behind her house before she left for an early shift. Now, there is a streetlight behind her house and as she opened her gate, a "tall man with fair hair" ran past. I sent an officer around to speak with her because she hadn't said which way he was going and I wanted further details, like his clothing, if she saw it. The direction was consistent with him coming from the hotel, but wasn't following the route which the dark-haired man took, so I think, intentionally or otherwise, they had split up. He startled her, so she recalled nothing except the original description she gave. She said she called it in just in case someone had been robbed nearby. The way the man was running looked as though he was afraid, rather than just late for work. Now, as evidence, it sucks, but if anyone else saw a fair-haired man in the small hours, then it could well support her story.'

McDonald paused for a second or two, 'You know André, I had let the second man in the robbery slip from my sight somewhat. Tunnel vision, I suppose. I agree it's not rock solid evidence, but yes, if you could dig a little more, it may be helpful. It would really tie the murderer into story, and it may be useful for Eli in future if he brings his spy ring to court.'

After a few pleasantries, he replaced the receiver. Eli was waiting impatiently, so he repeated what André had said.

Bernstein grinned, 'Great news. Most likely it will yield nothing, but it would certainly tie everything together if it were true. I guess Sallow is, if only temporarily, moved to the same, or higher, priority as 'Willow'. Oh, one last thing, if you speak to McDaid, I'd phrase it as 'when he gets the spy ring to court, not if.' Just a thought.'

McDonald laughed, 'I'd probably do that from simple self-preservation if I'm honest, Eli!'

Half an hour passed while McDonald made some notes. He had spent a great deal of time learning Pitman's shorthand, which had proven handy over the years. The ladies in the typing pool in London had scoffed at some of his errors but were secretly impressed.

He had just poured a last cup of coffee before he and Bernstein left to do a tour of the murder site when there was a knock at the door.

'Come in,' called Bernstein.

There was a momentary hesitation, then in walked Sullivan, the senior FBI man from the field office, and the young man who had been making notes at the briefing.

'Good afternoon gentlemen, we bring glad tidings. This is Special Agent Jackson.'

McDonald and Bernstein looked at each other, then back at the pair who had stopped just inside the door.

He turned to the young man next to him, 'Go ahead, Will, it was your catch.'

Looking a little nervous, the young man squared his shoulders.

'Well, sirs, something that Special Agent in Charge

Bernstein said in the briefing jogged my memory. I couldn't fix it in my mind, but I knew if I stopped thinking about it, then it would pop right in. Eventually it did: a few days ago we had a Portland man, who is a Professor at the Massachusetts Institute of Technology, fly in from Canada, where he had completed a lecture tour. He has just received an award in his field and there was a press photographer there to greet his flight.'

He reached into a satchel, which he had over his shoulder, and produced a well-read newspaper. Blushing, he spoke, 'My landlady saves newspapers for packing away her best crockery and such. Anyway, I retrieved this edition.'

Opening it on the table in front of Bernstein, the young man continued, 'Sir, look at the man behind the professor,' he stabbed a finger at the page.

McDonald moved over to Bernstein's desk and peered at the page. Behind a smiling man wearing a homburg hat and holding up a medal walked a dark-haired man with a small valise. His eyes widened.

The young man continued, 'This was the day after the robbery in Halifax, which you mentioned earlier, and the Professor travelled on the plane from Halifax. Anyway, I know a guy at the newspaper and went to see him. The reporter still had the negatives of that picture and he took three shots of the Professor. Two of them were of interest.'

He reached into his satchel again and spread out three photographs, one clearly an enlargement. In the enlargement, the man with the valise had a very obvious curved scar next to his left eye, and on the second image, he had put his hand up, as if scratching his temple.

'The enlargement is the best he can do, and cost me a bottle of bourbon, but I think it's worth it,' offered the youngster.

Bernstein glanced at Sullivan, who was beaming at the young man, then turned to the youngster with a grin, 'Young man, you will go far. How the hell did you remember this?' He gestured at the newspaper.

'Well, sir, it was pure chance. All I really remembered was the way his eyes were looking sideways at the camera. At the time I thought, "now there is a guy who doesn't like the Professor". I knew it was the camera capturing his face unflatteringly, of course, he probably only glanced over, but it was enough to hold it in my memory.'

Bernstein picked up the paper; the inferior quality of print did lend a fanatical sort of cast to Willow's face, 'Truly excellent work young man, well done.'

The young agent coloured and turned to his boss, who nodded.

'OK Jackson, the holiday is over. You can get back to work now. Once again, well done.'

As the young man left, Sullivan looked at Bernstein and McDonald, 'So what's the next step, gentlemen?'

Bernstein tapped a pencil on the table, 'We now have a resource to help track our man down. The question is, how do we use it? We have to get the enlarged picture wired to entry and exit points of the US, that is obvious. Here in Portland, do we put it in the newspaper under a headline reading "Have you seen this man?" or do we remain quiet?'

He looked at the other two and McDonald replied, 'While the direct approach to the public might yield intelligence and would certainly force him to remain in hiding, it could also trigger him to escape. As things stand, I would suggest a softer approach. We could show the picture to people at the airport and taxi drivers who will no doubt service new arrivals. In this way, we may not scare him into immediate action. If this approach turns nothing up, then we have a direct appeal as a backup. Any other thoughts?'

The other two men shook their heads, and Bernstein put his hand on Sullivan's shoulder, 'One thing we have to tell you Jim. We learned, from a source in Canada, that our blonde guy may be a part of the Nazi ring we're tracking. It's not firm evidence yet, but is a possibility. I'll update you on this if we get anything new, but I don't believe it's relevant, as yet, to the police department in their investigation. If you think it has become relevant, then don't wait. You have my full authority to tell them if needed, but impress upon them it's national security and highly classified, so they are to use the information on a need to know basis only. You OK with that?'

'I sure am. Listen, I'd better get back to the office otherwise Will Jackson will have solved the case and got my job! Be seeing you!' With a wave, he was gone.

Bernstein whistled, 'Are you as glad as I am that we learned about Portland? You should let your boss know about this. Might give him some ammunition to keep the big guy at the top of your pile off your case.'

'Absolutely, but first, let's look at the scene of the crime again, shall we? At least one thing is certain now. We are definitely on the trail of 'Willow'!

The two men sidled down the wharf and checked around the murder scene. The crates were gone, and they had scrubbed the ground to remove the blood. McDonald walked up the north-west side of the wharf, casting his eyes around as he walked. He stopped at a rope which was looped around an upright wooden beam, presumably a rubbing post for ships, given the posts were evenly spaced all the way along the wharf so far as he could see. The rope looked new, and he heaved on it, there was a considerable weight attached. He called Bernstein for a helping hand. As the two men hauled it from the water they could see it was a wicker creel of some sort. Once on the wharf Bernstein unwound a figure of eight of cord from a cleat which released a small door. McDonald peered in, 'We need to get this back in the water, Eli. The bloody thing is full of mussels, probably bait for long-lining or something.'

They secured the door and lowered away smartly. Once the rope hung tight again, they stepped back and looked around. McDonald's face cracked first, 'FBI interrogate shellfish in murder enquiry! Can you imagine if someone had seen us Eli?'

Eli sniffed his hands, 'My God, that basket stinks!'

They continued walking to the end and started back up

the wharf. There were the usual businesses and two larger lobster concerns with bigger buildings sporting freshly whitewashed wooden boards. As they reached the last of these two, McDonald stopped. There were a lot of cigarette butts on the floor just around the corner. Standing at the corner, he looked toward Commercial Street and raised an eyebrow.

'Eli, look here.' He pulled out his handkerchief and picked up two of the cigarette ends, one of which had the words 'Old Gold' printed diagonally up the end of the paper.

'I have a perfect view of the murder scene here, Eli. Also, there are no lights on this side of the building, so it would be a great place to watch at night. Notice that all these cigarette ends are fairly fresh.'

Eli peered around the corner himself, 'Sure is, but who was watching? Your man, the murderer, or a third party? Perhaps we should ask the owner of this business about these cigarette ends, it may be someone's place for a quiet smoke during working hours,' Bernstein led around to a door at the far end of the building, 'let me lead Horace.'

The door was unlocked, so Bernstein pulled it open and called out, 'Hello, anybody around?'

A voice from behind them said, conversationally, 'Sure is, can I help you?'

They turned to see a man in his late fifties or early sixties, 'Seth Dawson, I'm the owner here,' Mr Dawson held out his hand.

Bernstein showed his identification, and the man said

he'd already spoken to the police. Eli replied they had just found something at the corner they wanted to ask about. Seth accompanied them back to the corner and Eli asked if any of his people smoked.

'Sure do, but not out here. We have an open area on the other side of the building where people take their breaks. Big double doors which open on to the wharf for offloading the lobsters. Something else, though, this mess could only have been here for two days. Day before that we cleaned up a pile of seaweed and waste someone had dumped here and I checked the guys had done a decent job myself. No cigarette butts around that afternoon, no, sir.'

After allowing Seth to show them the break area, where one man was indeed smoking, they thanked him for his help and walked away.

They asked if Seth had a paper bag or small box, and a hand brush which they could use. Seth came out with them and Bernstein swept the rest of the cigarette ends into the brown paper bag. He noticed there were no matches, so whoever the smoker was, they had a lighter. They thanked Mr Dawson and walked off.

McDonald spoke once they were a reasonable distance from the business, 'So who was watching? Sallow, 'Willow,' or Mr Woodcock?'

That evening, they went out with one of Sullivan's men for a tour of every lowlife and informant who was willing to talk. They approached from the angle of the murder, rather than mention 'Willow' directly, and McDonald was under a strict injunction not to speak. His accent would attract too much comment from the people they were dealing with.

One known forger knew a tall blond-haired man who was known as a tough guy, but further enquiry by the field office showed he was currently in jail.

At eight-thirty, Bernstein suggested they reconvene the next day. He felt gritty and a little angry, so he sent the local guy home and invited McDonald to eat with him, an invitation gratefully accepted.

Bernstein said that he knew a place and after a twenty-minute walk they stood before a sign announcing the restaurant as the best place for lobster in Maine.

'Lobster, really? Are you trying to theme our day?' McDonald smiled.

'Three things Horace. One, the sign is one hundred percent accurate, two, the owner is Italian, so this place has his stamp on it and, three, I don't know anywhere else which will still be serving at this time on a weekday.'

McDonald laughed, 'A very persuasive argument Eli. Let's go in.'

They chose a table for two in the corner opposite the door and gratefully grabbed the menu, ordering a bottle of pinot grigio with two glasses, and a bowl of olives to start.

Bernstein took a sip of his wine before speaking in a hushed voice, 'So, overall, I think today has been a good day but I'm finding the lack of a lead, on what is almost definitely a local man, very frustrating.'

McDonald nodded, putting an olive stone on his side-plate, 'Absolutely, but here's a thought. We are, rightly, focussing on the criminal community because he has killed. However, if he is our second burglar, then he may be spying because of idealogical values, a need for money, or is being coerced in some way. In which case, he is not bound to have a criminal record.'

'Good point Horace, I hadn't thought of that. I just felt we were close and things were moving fast.'

'Well, they are. We've made such strides today, so let's not put a damper on it.'

The waiter came to take their order and brought a basket of bread. As he walked away McDonald said, 'Did you get anything back from the Captain of the Port before we left?

Bernstein briefly shook his head, 'No, I'll chase him up tomorrow morning, then get a signal to White Nab to come join the party.'

McDonald looked up, smiling, 'One thing we might need to establish well ahead of time is whether White Nab could stop and search any vessel suspected of aiding an escape or carrying stolen goods once in international waters. I would say that the US Coastguard could do this within US waters, but would there be legal or diplomatic implications if both ships left US waters, then a stop and search was performed. It may even need a warning shot or two to stop the vessel. Best to reach an accord before the fact, wouldn't you say?'

'Sure thing, Horace. I'll make some calls tomorrow.'

McDonald nodded, 'I'll tackle it from the British end too. I should also say, Eli, that you were right about the lobster!'

Next morning, Bernstein replaced the telephone handset in its cradle and rubbed his eyes. He had just arranged for White Nab to be berthed against a wharf near the harbour entrance and had asked the Captain of the Port to radio White Nab with instructions for berthing. He was just about to call Jack McDaid when there was a tap at the door and it opened. Sullivan poked his head around and grinned.

Bernstein waved him to enter, 'Come on in, Jim. What breakthrough has young Will made today?'

Sullivan smiled, 'I kept him busy yesterday, otherwise you'd have an envelope with the addresses of your suspects on your desk as we speak!'

McDonald was speaking to Sir Peter at his desk and waved a greeting at Sullivan, who continued, 'No, it's a different matter. One of my guys hails from Texas and he speaks very good Spanish. It occurred to me it might be useful if he is eating or drinking in the same bars the crew of the Posadilla are using. He's done a lot of surveillance in the past and avoids the usual give-aways.'

Bernstein nodded, 'That's a damned good idea Jim. Loose tongues and all that stuff. Also, we'll soon have access to some of the British ship's crew who can play the honest sailor and keep their eyes and ears open. Captain

McDonald tells me they are useful in all sorts of ways. I believe they had some rudimentary training, so I'm happy for you to use them under supervision.'

Sullivan grinned, 'The more numbers we have, the less likely they are to make us, so it sounds good to me. I'd better be getting back now. See you later.'

'Thanks Jim, much appreciated. Oh, not that I don't enjoy seeing you, of course, but did I give you my number?'

'You sure did, but it's the hot dog stand outside which really draws me here. So long!' With a wave he was gone, leaving Bernstein chuckling and shaking his head.

McDonald stood after his call ended and poured coffee. Bernstein thanked him and looked up inquisitively. McDonald put down the cup and spoke, 'The boss is much more confident that he can keep the wolves from our door now. I'm glad I caught him before his round of meetings. Also, he will speak to C, our leader, and have him establish rules of engagement for White Nab.'

'Oh, I wondered why you got in so early. I'm glad to hear he's happier.'

'How about you, Eli. Feeling more positive?'

'Yeah, slept like a log after a couple of glasses of wine. I'm on top form today.'

He updated McDonald on Sullivan's suggestion and looked at his wristwatch, 'I'll go to the police department now and listen in on the briefing. Oh, and I need to tell them about the cigarette butts and see if they can develop any fingerprints from them.' He picked up the paper bag with the evidence in it and left with a wave.

Chapter Eleven

43° 39' 29" N, 70° 15' 30" W

Portland, Maine

White Nab was at the northern end of her patrol route, around two miles south of Bald Head Cove, a wooded peninsular with a rocky shore. She was riding a slight swell as they turned to head south-west.

Nev Danby clambered up to the flying bridge and handed the Skipper a transcript of a radio message. Reading it, the Skipper nodded.

'Thanks Sparks, I'll nip down to the chart table and get you a time of arrival.'

Looking at the expectant faces of the lookouts, he grinned, 'Captain McDonald requests we proceed to Portland and berth near the harbour entrance. Looks like a run ashore, lads!' He left three beaming faces behind.

After five minutes at the chart table, the Skipper called

Nev, who popped his head out of the Wireless office. '
Sparks, can you call the Port Captain back and give our
E.T.A. As two hours from now?'

'Will do Skipper.'

The Skipper broke the good news to Arthur and Yorke,
who was sitting at his ASDIC set with an earphone over one
ear and a mug of tea in his hand.

The Skipper returned to the chart table, 'Arthur, bring
her onto to 242° compass would you?'

Arthur eased the wheel around then steadied her on the
new heading, '242° Skipper.'

'Thank you.' The Skipper picked up the intercom and
buzzed the flying bridge, 'Just keep a weather eye open for
small craft lads. There are a lot about in Casco Bay. Also,
you might see the Halfway Rock light, fine on the starboard
bow shortly. Let me know when it's abeam please.'

'Will do Skipper.'

Their passage was uneventful, and after rounding the
Ram Island Ledge Light, they altered to steer between
Cushing Island and the mainland. Once due west of
Catfish Rock they came up to 345° to clear Spring Point
Ledge.

They slowed slightly and gauged when to turn northwest
using a bearing on Fort Scammel. When a large jetty on
Peaks Island was open of a light at the north end of House
Island, they changed heading due west, into the harbour.

The harbour was the mouth of the Fore River, between
Portland to starboard and South Portland, with a short
breakwater on their port side.

The South Portland shore was lower and lightly wooded behind, with red-brick buildings inland of the foreshore. Northwest of the harbour, the buildings rose to a low hill. The Skipper noticed an enormous, yet elegant, spire which he assumed would be a large church or cathedral. Ahead, he could dimly make out a bridge across the channel. He and Arthur used glasses to identify their berth and Arthur asked Pickering to make ready the Q flag.

As they approached, they swung round and manoeuvred in astern, in case they needed to leave quickly. There was very little tidal flow and what there was, pushed them toward the wharf where a white-hatted man stood waiting.

Once secured, the young man came onboard and checked all the guns were unloaded and covered, and that the ammunition was secured. Arthur showed him that all depth charges were in the safe position. After checking their papers, he gave directions to the office where they could get help if needed, then handed over an envelope for the Skipper before leaving with a cheery wave.

The Skipper asked his officers to convene in his cabin once they had cleared away and set a harbour watch for security. He reminded Number One and Arthur that the lads who did harbour watch in New York were to be first for a brief run ashore.

Sitting in his cabin, he read the note which simply said, 'please call this number when you arrive, H'. He went out on deck to find Arthur and two deckhands using a fresh water hose to sluice down the deck. Number One had some hands painting on the afterdeck. He called over to Arthur that he needed to make a telephone call and would come straight back. He gave a big wink to Peter Boulby, 'Unless I find a pub on the way Peter, eh?'

Boulby grinned, 'Get one in for me Skipper.'

With a wave, the Skipper strolled off. The wind was freshening, and he smelled rain, so he suspected Arthur would stop the wash-down as soon as he realised. He sped up on his way to the small office at the landward end of the wharf, as he hadn't worn an overcoat. Once inside, he asked to use the telephone and dialled the number on his note.

'McDonald here,' came the quick reply.

'Hello sir, it's the Skipper. Just letting you know we're on the wharf now and awaiting orders.'

'Righto Skipper. It's probably best if I come to you. It'll be twenty minutes to half an hour before I get there.'

'No problem sir, shall I wait onboard or in the office?'

'Onboard Skipper, especially if you have some malt left!'

'I think I can swing that sir, no problem.'

The Skipper had moved his meeting with his officers into the aft cabin, where there was more room than in his own, Billy had brought in some tea, and the Skipper chatted with Arthur and Number One. When Svein had arrived, they discussed the plans for maintenance, harbour watches, and runs ashore. As the officers were leaving, Fred, their extra watch keeper, brought Captain McDonald down to the cabin.

McDonald shook hands with them all and turned to the Skipper, 'No need for everyone to leave on my account, Skipper. I can brief you all at once if it helps?'

'Fine by me sir, you lads can stick around unless you have anything pressing to attend to.'

Arthur tapped the intercom to tell Fred they would be in the cabin for a while longer if needed, then sat on the vee-shaped padded settle, which roughly followed the shape of the stern around the back of a similarly shaped dining table.

Billy dropped in with tea for McDonald, in the usual tin mug, naturally.

McDonald took a sip then spoke, 'Skipper, I assume you've briefed these gentlemen about my mission here?'

The Skipper nodded, 'I have sir, yes.'

'Good. Well, it seems we are in the right place. We have received definite confirmation that the man who escaped from Halifax disembarked from an aircraft here in Portland. Luckily, for us, he was visible in the background of a photograph of a local celebrity arriving at the airport. One of our FBI colleagues was sharp enough to recall the image in a newspaper, and confirmed when and where it was shot, so there is no doubt we are geographically close. I say that because, while we're in the right place, we have no further sightings of the man we've given the code name 'Willow' to give us a lead on his whereabouts. All is not lost, however. Sadly, a British agent was murdered after asking questions about a dark-haired man with a scar. This is a setback, of course, but it may have given us new information. Our man 'Willow' seems to be a professional, yet there have been several incongruities which point to another person being involved. Now this person, described as a big blonde haired man, was the one who killed the agent according to a witness, and there is circumstantial evidence he is a local. We're calling him Sallow. So, we may therefore have found a weak link in the network, of which 'Willow' is a part. We decided that, given his lack of professionalism, and the hard truth that Willow remains invisible, we are better served by searching for him rather than 'Willow'. Questions so far?'

McDonald looked around and the Skipper lifted a finger, 'If your man 'Willow' has disappeared, isn't there a chance that he may have already gone, sir?'

McDonald smiled, 'Good question Skipper. I had the same worry myself, but we have evidence they are waiting instructions. I can't say much more than that, but it is solid information, so we think he's unlikely to have left. We're working with the FBI on this, so we're not just guessing, though to be frank, a lot of intelligence work is little more than educated guessing! I have to say that there would be severe repercussions internationally if Germany learned the US are helping us like this, so keep it among ourselves. America also has internal law protecting their neutrality, so we must tread carefully. I should also say we have approached the Captain of the Port here, and there were no ships which left in the period between 'Willow' turning up and our own arrival. This, however, brings me to my main point. A Spanish freighter arrived two days ago and we need to monitor her in case they get the missing item aboard and take off. We are desperately short of people and we'd like to borrow a few of your crew to man an observation post, which the FBI has set up in an empty office on the top floor of a building at the end of Moulton Street. There will be no involvement with any efforts to intercept or arrest, we just need sharp eyes and the ability to stay awake. Guess which crew that reminded me of!'

There was a ripple of laughter around the room.

McDonald continued, 'So I'll need a couple of men and an officer. There are two cot beds in the building, so I'd like two men doing turn and turn about in the observation post with an officer on standby here in case of problems. The other cot bed will house an FBI agent on standby. Now, there is another element to this. What if S.S. Posadilla, the Spanish ship, sets sail? Well, we are awaiting some rules of engagement from Blighty, but they will need to get approval from the United States so that we don't breach their neutrality. We don't expect problems and I have spoken to the management in SIS to make sure it's actioned quickly. We can't make this up on the hoof.'

The Skipper coughed, 'I assume the rules you mention are to stop the vessel outside of territorial waters sir?'

McDonald nodded, 'Yes, but we just need to be sure how far you can go. Frankly, if they're helping the Nazis, I'd say we should sink them, but that may not be palatable to

Whitehall and, from my point of view, we wouldn't have positive confirmation that the stolen item was actually on board.'

Arthur lifted a finger, 'Do we need to keep the boiler warm for a quick departure, sir? I'm just wondering if we need to top up the bunkers before we're needed.'

McDonald looked at the Skipper, who shrugged, 'Arthur's right, sir. Better we top up than regret it later, I'd say. Also, it might be hard to see if the Spaniard raises steam at night, so I think we should keep our boiler warm for a fairly quick departure.'

Shrugging his shoulders, McDonald smiled, saying, 'OK, I'll ask my FBI contact to speak with the Captain of the Port about a bunkering facility for you. Also, judging from what you say, I'll ask that the duty officer alerts the FBI field office if the Posadilla leaves, or prepares to do so. Naturally, the FBI will get a message to you.'

The Skipper nodded as Svein said, 'We'll keep the firebox and feedwater warm Skipper. No problem. I'll let the firemen know we'll be coaling soon, they'll be delighted.'

McDonald looked bemused, so the Skipper leaned toward him, 'The coal goes down the scuttles, you may have seen the covers on deck, and it tends to form a heap in the bunkers. Our firemen are also trimmers, and have to move it about so that it sits fairly level and is less likely to shift, which would change the ship's trim. Also, as we use it, they use a watertight tunnel from the engine room up to the bunkers to shift it about if they've used more from one side or other of the cross bunkers.'

McDonald smiled, 'Thank you Skipper, I did wonder. I'll be off now, but I'll send an FBI man around this evening to move the first shift in. Let me know if you have any issues.'

Goldstein started as his telephone jangled loudly. He picked up the receiver, and his eyebrows raised as he recognised David, his second in command at the listening post near Ponkapoag.

'Hi David, what's the news from Boston?'

'Well sir, we just had a hit on one of the frequencies you asked us to monitor. It was a strange transmission exchange, that's for sure. We picked up an encrypted signal from Europe. Our guys have had a try at decrypting, but with no success, unfortunately. So far, so ordinary ; here's the odd part, however. A signal went back, the same awful morse as the last signal, in *plain language*, and was repeated three times, with no response! It staggered us, I can tell you.'

Bernstein nodded as he held the receiver, 'David, we have experienced several things in this case which smack of a ten-year-old being behind them. Signalling skills is only one of them. We veer from extreme professionalism to this kind of crap. It's confusing, but we suspect a pro-German U.S. Citizen who wants to play on their side is involved, somehow. They must be desperate to use him at all, but it's all our team here in Portland can think of to explain what's going on. I wonder, if we really stretched our imagination, we might imagine an American ham radio operator replying to a strange signal...'

'I don't think so, boss. The morse was so poor that any self respecting ham radio enthusiast would be embarrassed. In fact he would be unlikely to pass the license test! Also, we're way out of the normal ham radio bands here. I have nothing a court would accept, of course, but in terms of professional radio communication, I think your first suggestion is more likely. And it was definitely the same person who sent all three replies. We can tell from the keying.'

Bernstein bit his lip, 'OK David, good work and please keep monitoring those frequencies. Also, could you send an accurate transcript of the original message from Europe to me? I'll need it as quickly as possible, so please use a courier,' he gently replaced the receiver.

He made some notes and was getting coffee as McDonald came into the office, followed by Gloria, who was on a mission to stop them drinking stale coffee. As Gloria left, Bernstein spoke, 'I have news Horace.'

He quickly brought McDonald up to speed, pausing as Gloria swished back in with the coffee jug.

As Gloria left, McDonald's thanks ringing after her, he turned to Bernstein, 'Well, as you say, it still seems to fit very well with our ideas about the second man being unprofessional.'

Special Agent Billy Joe Havers tapped the ash from his cigarette and sipped his beer. He sat in a cubicle near the pool table but facing away from the Spanish sailors shooting pool. It was too easy to be seen looking at them and anyway, all he needed was to hear them speak.

For the most part, it was raucous tales of drinking bouts in ports all over the world with an occasional, and probably imaginary, story of sexual prowess. In among the rubbish were some grains of gold dust, however. He'd repeatedly heard them complain they should be homeward bound by now, and one man said he missed Vigo. It was not clear whether that was to be their next stop, final destination, or his home, but it reinforced the earlier complaints.

Today had been special. A few minutes before, one of the Spaniards, who seemed less able to take his drink, had blurted loudly, 'Why do we wait for some sauerkraut eater, we should go!' He had been immediately hushed by his shipmates, but Billy Joe knew this was indeed gold. He also knew he had to get this to the office quickly.

As he stood, a sailor bumped his elbow and started yelling about the American steer who couldn't see in front of his face. Billy Joe kept his smile fixed and, speaking in English, said 'Pardon me, friend, I didn't see y'all coming.' As the man kept jabbing his finger at him, Billy Joe allowed some annoyance to show across his face. Some of the other sailors came over to him and apologised in Spanish, so he shrugged his shoulders and said, 'Sorry guys, I don't understand, but I think I guess your meaning.' He held out his hand and the first man who had apologised shook it. As Billy Joe left, he saw the barkeep walking back to the pool table with a short cudgel in the back of his waistband.

McDonald was making notes while he waited for Bernstein to reappear from 'the john' as he, slightly opaquely, called the lavatory. The door abruptly burst open and Jim Sullivan strode in, clutching a large brown-paper bag.

'Captain McDonald! Nice to see you again, would you care for a hot dog?'

'Do you know, I rather think I do, Mr Sullivan,' he smiled.

'Jim will do just fine, sir. Here you go.'

Bernstein walked and grinned hugely as he smelled the delicious aroma.

'Jim, you are a real morale booster.'

Sullivan grinned, 'Well, I ain't hardly started yet sir,' he said, in a very fake hick accent.

Bernstein groaned, 'Do go on, Jim. But in your normal voice, for pity's sake!'

Grinning again, Sullivan continued, 'You're no fun. At least Captain McDonald laughed.'

McDonald held up his hand, speaking through a mouthful of frankfurter, 'Whatever accent you like, Jim. I won't criticise a man who brings manna from heaven.'

Sullivan smiled beatifically, 'At last, a man of taste,' his voice changed to businesslike, 'So here, gentlemen, is the real morale booster. I bring confirmation that the

Spanish ship is waiting to take onboard a "sauerkraut eater" according to an alcohol related slip in a bar, where my Texan Special Agent was on hand to hear it. The exact phrase, spoken in Spanish, was "Why do we wait for some sauerkraut eater, we should go!" So how about that?'

'Outstanding!' Bernstein grinned widely as McDonald clapped Sullivan on the back.

'So, barring a massive coincidence, it's possible one or more of our Nazis are attempting to get back to Europe. This is, in one sense, encouraging; although it's more likely they're waiting for him to deliver something for them to ship east rather than leaving himself. If that's the case I'd lay odds that I know what it is!'

Bernstein stroked his chin, 'Yeah, I think it's the latter suggestion Horace, and I wouldn't bet against you on what they'll be wanting to ship!'

They both turned after a knock at the door, Bernstein calling, 'Come in!'

Simmons opened the door and hung up his hat on a stand in the corner.

'Hello Peter, what can I do for you?' McDonald said, with a wave to a chair by his desk.

'Hello, sir. My FBI contact, Special Agent Lightfoot, and I may have dug something up. We have, quietly, been speaking to cab drivers on the airport run and we may have a lead. One driver dropped a fare off, a man with dark hair and moustache, carrying a small suitcase. The drop was in Atlantic Street, on Munjoy Hill, but doesn't recall the house number. We never mentioned the suitcase publicly, so we think this is worth following up.'

McDonald's eyes sparkled, 'Well done to you both Simmons, well done indeed!'

'Thank you, sir. Now, I reason that, if it were me on the run, I'd get dropped off and then walk to my destination. Lightfoot is with the driver as we speak and they will drive up Atlantic Street to see if the cabbie can recall the drop off point. We think we can use that as a centre point for our search. Jim Sullivan has whipped up three guys to do casual strolls to look for likely places, any boarded up or neglected properties, for example. They will walk in figure-eight patterns to avoid the same man being seen too often. With your permission, sir, I'd like to go up there myself.'

McDonald glanced at Bernstein, who nodded before replying. 'Of course, Peter, but please do remember what this man, or these men, are capable of. I understand completely that you want to apprehend them for killing Gordon Woodcock, but please, don't let's end up with another dead colleague.'

Simmons smiled bitterly, 'Sir, I'll be honest. I'd like to kneel them down and shoot them in the head, but I wouldn't be in this job if I didn't believe in the primacy of law, and in democracy. So no, with regret, I shall not go wild west on you.'

McDonald looked in his eyes and saw only sadness and

determination, no trace of anger, or, worse, the controlled deadpan of a man hiding his intentions.

'Alright Peter, please join the team, but there is one thing.'

'Sir?'

'You missed all the booze-ups from your list of reasons to join the service.'

Simmons laughed, 'Plus all the nights spent out in the rain, sir. Don't forget that little joy. Right, I'll be going then.'

As the door closed, Bernstein smiled, 'Looks like we've found another promising man there Horace.'

'I think so Eli, time will tell how he deals with his feelings after this operation is over, though. Nevertheless, I wish him well and will monitor his progress.'

Chapter Twelve

43° 39' 29" N, 70° 15' 30" W

Portland, Maine

The day was mostly drab and cool weather-wise, but occasional breaks in the cloud highlighted the autumnal colours in the trees, many already shedding some leaves. An FBI colleague who was doing a drive-by survey of houses on nearby streets dropped Peter Simmons and Special Agent Lightfoot off. Their idea was that on the next garbage collection, the following day, they would have a man or two on the truck which would give them an opportunity to inspect properties which were disused and identify any which had generated no waste, indicating their owners were not at home. This was a first pass, to look for obvious candidates. Simmons' first impression was of attractive, if occasionally run-down, wood-frame houses and a mixture of architectural styles.

Peter and Simon each clutched an encyclopaedia to give the impression they were doorstep sales agents, a cover which explained them looking at every property as they passed. They planned walking up Atlantic Street together. They were to slow down as they passed the area which the taxi driver had identified as the drop off point, then would split up at the junction with Congress Street. Simmons would then turn right, going back downhill on Munjoy Street. Lightfoot would turn left and descend on St Lawrence Street. Later, they would each go two blocks out from where their partner had stopped and work back in to the area already covered. This would maximise the time between each individual passing the same point. By six p.m. They had covered a wide area southeast of Congress Street, out to where the driving survey, which had covered the area northwest of Congress Street, had started. Their total haul of visibly empty properties was only three, but they had hopes the garbage truck survey would be more revealing.

Simmons reported back to McDonald at six-thirty. The outcome was as they had both expected, but a result on the next day would be more revealing.

McDonald smiled as he replaced the receiver. Glancing up at Bernstein, he said, 'Progress, as expected, Eli. They've had a clever idea of checking which houses might appear lived in, but without its owners present, by riding on a garbage truck and looking for empty dustbins. Ingenious!'

Bernstein's mouth twitched, 'Yeah, Jim just told me. I suspect it was his idea. Listen, Horace, while we're speaking, the guys from my intercept site have sent me a transcript of the coded message they received, you know, the one which prompted the amateurish guy to keep asking for repeats?'

McDonald nodded.

'Well, you'll be aware that SIS, or the Government Code and Cypher School, made an offer for intelligence sharing last June. What you may not know is that the decision to turn down the offer was led by the Navy. The Army, and some big names in our government, took a different view. Anyway, we think you, as in Britain, may have the ability to decrypt this message. Would you be willing to talk to whoever can help? We need every scrap of information we can get and, as your delegation made clear, there are advantages both ways if we can rekindle discussion on the intelligence sharing.'

McDonald pursed his lips, 'Well, I'm not sure what you're referring to dear boy,' this was a lie, and they both knew it, 'but I shall certainly pass on your request. I recommend you send it to Stephenson in New York. The BSC have a teleprinter, I believe.'

'Of course, Horace. Thank you. Changing the subject, the old RDF set and my man with the newer one will arrive in the morning. They're still listening from Boston, but if we can get the set installed on your ship, we'll have a great asset, right where it's needed.'

McDonald made a brief note, 'Thank you, Eli. Now, the chief engineer on White Nab is a genius, and they have a very competent wireless operator. Will they be able to install the equipment?'

'Sure, I think they would be fine, but my guy can help too, if needed.'

'Thanks, Eli. I'll nip down shortly and let the Skipper know. Can you man the phones for an hour?'

'Sure thing, Horace.'

It surprised the Skipper to see McDonald's head pop up over the top of the ladder.

'Hello, sir. What brings you to our ocean greyhound?'

'Good news, Skipper. This greyhound is about to get an upgrade. Mr Bernstein has some outdated, but still useful, equipment to give you a radio direction finding capability. We think it may come in handy for tracking down our spy.'

'That does sound useful, sir.'

'Indeed, I understand their man will arrive soon, and I'll bring him down. If I'm busy, perhaps you could send Number One to escort him, or pop up yourself if you prefer. Whoever comes should appear in civilian dress, though. Our office is in a department store and our cover is thin enough as it is!'

The Skipper smiled, 'I understand, sir. We'll try to blend in. I just hope they understand Yorkshire, that's all.'

'Probably more than they understand me, Skipper.'

They both laughed.

'Have you got time for some tea, sir?'

'I haven't, Skipper. I promised Mr Bernstein I'd get back quickly, and I need to make a call of my own, unfortunately.'

'Next time then, sir. Until then, I'd better get back to helping Svein sort out the light in our compass repeater.'

With a wave, McDonald was gone.

Two days later, McDonald and Bernstein were at their desks. Rain was hammering the window from outside, and their mood seemed to reflect the miserable weather.

McDonald rarely smoked, but today he allowed himself a cigar. It seemed like a day for cheering himself up.

The last couple of days had been efficient, if not resoundingly successful. They had completed their survey of the area where a taxi had dropped Willow, and had discovered one house which seemed occupied, yet had no waste. They had discretely surrounded the house until a neighbour came outside and asked what they were doing. The ensuing conversation revealed that the owners had gone upstate to visit a relative and had only been gone for two days. He himself had emptied the small amount of trash in their can into his own, to save him having to carry two trashcans to the kerbside. They dispersed their men as quietly as possible, and asked the gentleman not to tell his neighbours as they were seeking a fugitive who might still be in the area and they didn't want to warn him they were looking.

White Nab now had a loop antenna which could rotate to determine where a signal was coming from. The FBI operative from Boston had helped them set it up and had helped them check it over. The Skipper's wireless operator, Nev, had practiced using commercial stations, and briefed the officers on how the unit functioned. Svein had repacked the deck-head seal after Nev had reported a small leak: not ideal with lots of fairly high voltage transformers in the wireless office. All of which was marvellous, except there had been no signals transmitted for them to receive. Nothing except static from all the frequencies they monitored. The Skipper had asked Nev to train a couple of crew members, one of whom was the first officer, on how to use the homing setup. They didn't need to write the signal down. Only yell out to the watch keeper for a note of the ship's position and speed. They then recorded the ship's heading from a compass repeater installed on the wall and the bearing of the signal. This would allow them to calculate the actual bearing from the position they had heard it. There was certainly some error built in, but over the distance they were likely to be from the sender, it ought to be good enough. Yet the sender remained silent.

McDonald drained the rest of his coffee, glancing across at Bernstein, who was looking at something through a magnifying glass.

'Are you going for the Sherlock Holmes look yourself, Eli?' he said, grinning despite his desperate mood.

Bernstein flashed a tiny smile but carried on peering,

'Horace, c'mon over and look. I found a sticker or something on the enlarged photo from the airport.'

'A sticker?' asked McDonald.

'Sure, or maybe a repair. I'm certain there is lettering on it but it's just too indistinct for me to make the words out. Could you take a look, please?'

McDonald took the glass, after five minutes of study he also admitted defeat.

'It's so close to resolving, but I just can't quite make it out. What about asking the photographer to make it readable?'

Bernstein shook his head, 'Well, I'd say no. Young Jackson said this is the best the photographer can do, but also, please recall, he is a press photographer. The last thing we need now is for this to hit the newsstands, which it might if he thinks there's a bigger story. Also, I guess that anything on the outside of his suitcase wouldn't be something he'd like to keep secret.'

'I was thinking it might hint to recent whereabouts, but if that's the best enlargement we can get, it's a fool's errand, anyway.' McDonald sighed.

Bernstein tapped his teeth with a pencil, 'Hey, look. I'm thinking…' he trailed off into silence.

McDonald glanced at him, but Berstein shook his head, 'I must be tired. I was thinking about airport left luggage, but he had his case in the cab.'

'When I find myself at a dead end, I normally go for a stroll in St James' Park. What would you say to a walk down to the waterfront? I need to check with the Skipper how things are going with his lads in the observation post, anyway.'

'Yeah, sure, I'll go to the observation post itself, if it's clear for me to enter. I understand they have keys to a door on the opposite side of the building now, so it's easier to get in unobserved. I'll ask Sullivan to call ahead.'

Half an hour later, McDonald sat in the Skipper's cabin alongside the Skipper and Arthur. Holding a mug of tea, he was watching a dancing spectre of brightness reflected through the port light from the water outside. A thump on the deckhead and a clank on the stair from the wheelhouse heralded the arrival of Number One.

'Apologies Gentlemen, I was just checking off the spares inventory with Svein and we were only a few minutes for completing a very long list!'

McDonald smiled, thinking how the young man now had the confidence in his self and his crew to be less formal.

'Not a problem at all. Please, do sit down. There's some tea for you over there.'

'Thank you, sir.' Number One gratefully gulped some tea.

'Well, chaps I wanted to pass on some information which was relayed through my boss regarding rules of engagement. This only comes into play if the Spanish ship departs, and we have evidence she has the missing item on board. The instructions are actually quite simple, you can do nothing to inhibit her progress, or board her, as long as you're in United States territorial waters. Once you're in international waters, however, you are at liberty to use your own discretion on the best way to stop her. His Majesty's government are content to pick up the diplomatic shrapnel afterwards if necessary. It's very much as expected, and I assume that is clear enough?'

The Skipper nodded thoughtfully, 'Definitely sir. Could anybody supply us with photographs of the vessel? I'm wondering where the wireless office is and the speed with which they could send a message. Actually, our chaps in the observation post might well be able to tell us without bothering to take pictures.'

'Yes, Skipper. Please ask them to get that information for you if they don't already have it. I assume that you'll be able to do a limited amount of forward planning if you know where the radio operator is?'

'Exactly, sir. If the wireless Office is separate, behind the bridge, for example, then a well-placed round from our twelve pounder might solve the problem. If events justified that course of action, naturally. Alternatively, if we boarded her, it would be good to know where we're going. I don't suppose that we could get a man in the water, armed with some wire hawser to wrap around her propeller, could we? That might stop the escape before it even starts.'

'Good idea, Skipper. I'll have a word with Mr Bernstein and get his view on whether it's likely to succeed. Again, your chaps on the scene may already have some insight into that. I'm told there is access to the observation post from the opposite side of the building from SS Posadilla, so perhaps Number One or yourself could take a walk over there toward dusk this evening?'

'Yes, sir. We can certainly sort that out.'

After waving to Gloria, who was deep in conversation on the telephone, McDonald pushed open the door to their office.

'Hello Eli. How's things?'

'Pretty good, thank you, Horace. Apart from the ninety-nine percent of things that are awful of course.'

'So, your day sounds very similar to my own.'

They both laughed as McDonald headed for the coffeepot.

'I've just come from White Nab and I wanted to get your view on a plan that the Skipper and his officers came up with. They are wondering if they could get a man in the water to wrap a steel hawser around the Spanish ship's propeller. In that way, as soon as he moves the shaft, it would tangle and stop the ship from leaving. At least for a while.' He deposited fresh coffee on Bernstein's desk.

Bernstein thought for a minute or two before replying, 'I can't recall how easy it would be to get into the water unseen, but the most important element is that they risk getting caught.'

'Yes, it crossed my mind as well. I know the Skipper and his crew are sensible and very pragmatic. At the moment, they plan to ask their men helping in the observation post whether or not it's feasible.'

'Fair enough, Horace. Let's see whether they still think the plan is workable after speaking to their colleagues. If they do, I'll go to Jack McDaid and run the plan past him.'

McDonald smiled and nodded, 'Thank you, Eli, you're very kind.'

Bernstein shrugged, 'Hey, no problem. So, I've spoken to the intercept station, but there are no signs of activity on the frequencies they're monitoring. It's so frustrating, yet I can't imagine they will stay silent for much longer.'

'Hope so, Eli. I have to be honest, there is a large part of me that's fearing our friend Willow may have already left the United States. I know it doesn't explain the actions of an idiot, repeatedly asking for further transmissions, but I would expect there to have been some change or movement by now. For all, I know they're already dissecting the damn thing in Berlin.'

'Hey Horace, you've got the night terrors again, my friend. Given what the agent heard in the bar, they are clearly waiting for someone of German origin. I can't imagine a neutral freighter captain would be willing to wait this long if the only agent, or at least the only one we know of, in the area has already left.'

'Unless it's a ruse to get us looking in the wrong direction, dear boy. I fear things may be more bleak than we realise, I'm afraid.'

'Listen, let's finish early then go grab a decent meal and a couple of beers. I think we need a pick me up.'

Chapter Thirteen

43° 39' 29" N, 70° 15' 30" W

Portland, Maine

The following morning, both men reported in bright and early, having slept well and enjoyed the meal.

Bernstein positively beamed at McDonald, 'So, how's your positivity level this morning, Horace?'

'Higher than yesterday, but by no means record-breaking. You?'

'Record-breaking my friend, record-breaking. I think it's high time we sat ourselves down and reviewed where we are, and what our options are right now.'

'I couldn't agree more, Eli. A damn fine idea.'

Bernstein tapped the tabletop with a pencil, 'Okay, let's slay the ogre in the room before we move on. Yes, the network has gone quiet, but I don't agree that means they've accomplished their mission. So, why do you think that? I hear you ask. Well, we had a solid lead on Munjoy Hill, which led us nowhere. Boo-hoo, let's just deal with it. Portland is a big place, so if we hadn't found the cabbie, where would we be looking right now? I'd suggest that the next logical step would be to quietly look at hotels, especially the cheaper flophouse type of establishment. It's much easier for a guy to disappear, or at least not have to answer questions, in that kind of place.'

McDonald shrugged, 'I suppose so, I certainly don't think it would do any harm. Maybe we could use the police department with as few of Sullivan's FBI team as possible?'

Bernstein reached for his telephone, saying, 'Sure thing, let's get that organised now and see if we can get results quickly.'

Later that day, a Police Lieutenant and young Will Jackson of the FBI had pushed two tables together and spread a large street plan of Portland. Using a telephone directory and a list the Police held, they were marking off the location of every hotel and boarding house which fitted the bill. The Lieutenant marked half a dozen places in red pen. These were locations he and his officers felt were the most likely places Willow could hide.

Back in their own office, both Bernstein and McDonald spoke again, and agreed the hotels had to be checked in the interest of a thorough investigation, however, they both had a feeling that nothing would come of the search.

'As I said before, Eli, by doing the groundwork in this way, we increase confidence in any leads we might get going forward.'

Bernstein tapped his teeth, 'I can't help thinking, Horace that the network has gone quiet because they know we are pursuing them. I mean, they would've known we'd be looking, but I suspect they now know we're looking in the right place. I think both of us would go dark on communications if we were in that position, yes?'

'Yes, definitely. So, do you think there is a way to force them to transmit again?'

'Sure, there'll be a way alright, we just need to figure out what it is.'

McDonald frowned, his eyes distant, 'Alright, let's think logically about this. I think we both still agree that the idea of one professional and one rank amateur working together is the most likely scenario, given the facts as we know them. We also believe that a more developed network would be better manned, and would have communications and other procedures in place already.'

Bernstein nodded, 'That makes sense to me.'

'Good. Now, we're almost certain that Sallow is new to the game, and Willow has shown us he is a very capable operator. I'm thinking of his escape from the hotel where the burglary took place, and his ability to evade our search. However, there is, I imagine, a very strong chance that this wasn't a pre-arranged plan. Thinking back to the strange security arrangements put in place by the security service back in England, I wonder if the Nazi network didn't expect there to be any better security at the hotel. I can't imagine why. They must've known that we had nabbed their foot-soldiers in Euston Station, but it occurs to me they would expect that operation to be carried out by the security service, rather than the secret intelligence service. That might explain why they had the idea that, because the next stop was on foreign soil, the security would be pretty lax. If I'm right, then what we've been looking at ever since then isn't cunning, master-plan, but a hastily cobbled together escape, albeit with one person involved who knows the game.'

Bernstein tapped the table, 'All of which is very interesting, and possibly correct, but what good does it do for us, Horace?'

McDonald looked down at the floor, 'Well, not very much I suppose. Although, did we ever get a more detailed description of Osier from the agents who were monitoring the dead letter drop? I suppose there's a tiny chance that some detail they noticed might interest us.'

Bernstein frowned, 'Oh, good point. The New York FBI office was going to follow up on that. Leave it with me, Horace.' He strode over to his desk and began leafing through his notebook. After a few minutes, he located the number he needed.

'Horace, I'll need to do this on a secure line, so I'll take a walk down to the field office. It shouldn't take me too long and I'll come straight back and brief you when I'm done.'

McDonald, making notes himself, glanced up. 'No problem, Eli. Speak soon.'

With the office empty, McDonald decided to chase up the potential decryption of the signal which was received from Germany. He wasn't expecting too much from it, but it was worth the effort given their current lack of hard information. After a few minutes on the telephone with the BSC in New York, he was told that he had received a secure signal from SIS. They promised a delivery, direct to him, using a BSC courier in the next twenty-four hours.

An hour later, Bernstein came back with a very odd look on his face. He pulled a chair from the next desk along and sat at the end of McDonald's desk.

'Well, Horace, that was an eye opener, I can tell you! It appears the New York office decided to drop our project almost as soon as we left. Horace, it's beyond comprehension and Jack McDaid is, well, you know him, I don't think any of those guys will get much sleep tonight. It turns out that the team doing surveillance on the dead letter drop was taking photographs of anyone approaching the drop, using a powerful telescopic lens. They were hidden in the groundskeepers shack some distance away.'

McDonald's jaw dropped, 'Dear God, that's incredible! To be fair, it's probably no worse than Paterson's actions so, no hard feelings!'

Bernstein smiled mirthlessly, 'Yeah, well, McDaid has clarified that prints of every photograph will be on my desk before ten a.m. tomorrow, or there will be some career terminations before five p.m. However, and, I'm guessing, out of self defence, the team leader has described the person who left the letter in the drop as a well-built blonde-haired man. It wasn't Bauer! How the hell this information didn't get to us I will never know, but I can tell you that by close of business tomorrow, Jack will know, and those responsible won't believe the whirlwind they have created!'

McDonald's face had visibly brightened, 'So, Sallow is the same person as Osier, it seems! I suppose this shrinks the network and points to it being less of a threat, at least for the moment. This may go nowhere, Eli, but I do have a good feeling about it.'

Both Bernstein and McDonald were in their office at seven-fifteen the following day. They made coffee and McDonald had brought in a breakfast bagel for each of them.

Everything was quiet until eight-thirty, when Gloria popped her head through the door and said, 'Courier for Mr Bernstein.'

Bernstein smiled, 'Thank you, Gloria. Send them in if you would.'

Waiting for Gloria to leave, Bernstein pointed to a desk near his own, 'On here please.'

The man placed the box down; it was clearly very heavy and was large. As the door closed, Bernstein showed his identification badge, signed for the delivery, then confirmed the FBI office from which they had sent the box. The Courier nodded and quietly left. They could faintly hear him, thanking Gloria as he passed her desk.'

When he opened the box, he discovered brown paper parcels with a date marked upon each one. The parcel with the dates of the pickup was asterisked and this one he opened. Spreading around ten photographs on to the table, it was immediately obvious that the last four were taken much closer together, and revealed the man looking back, before reaching into the waste can. The last two images showed him turn face-on to the camera with the last image, showing him striding closer to the camera as he pushed the envelope into his pocket.

McDonald, peering past Bernstein's arm, whistled, 'Well, if we can't get an identification from those photos, I'll be struck dumb!'

Eli nodded, smiling, 'I guess we should hotfoot it to the Police Department and set up a comparison with similar looking men from mugshots. The weak link may be our witness, but let's see if he's sober.'

McDonald grimaced, 'Eli, may I leave that with you, please? I am expecting some information which may be of use and I'm guessing the police might ask questions if I'm too involved.'

'Good point, Horace. See you later.'

McDonald leaned back in his chair, massaging his temples. It suddenly felt like they had gained momentum. All his professional sensors told him that the endgame was approaching.

Chapter Fourteen

43° 39' 29" N, 70° 15' 30" W

Portland, Maine

Bernstein perched on the edge of a desk, watching the tableau before him. Bernie Tasker, their drink addled witness, was held in a cell and plied with coffee and water for two hours, but was now passably sober. They had laid out eight photographs of well-built, blonde-haired individuals, and Tasker was studying them carefully. Eli was fretting. Tasker really didn't seem to have a decisive opinion. After five minutes of poring, he leaned back in his chair. The Police Officer sitting opposite leaned forward, 'Well?'

'Oh, it's this one,' Tasker jabbed a grubby fingernail on the photo from New York, 'no doubt about that, Officer. I was just looking to see if I recognised anyone else...'

Bernstein stood and leaned over Tasker, scooping up the photos. As he walked away, he turned.

'It maybe a joke to you, Tasker, but you're the only one in this room who finds this funny.'

The police chief waved Bernstein toward his office.

'We might have problems with this one come the day of the trial, assuming we get that far. I think I'll get my boys to pick him up a couple of days early and we can dry him out before he gives evidence.'

'I wouldn't disagree with you there Chief. Please accept my thanks for the work you and your boys are putting in. I think we're getting close to finding our culprit now.'

He waved as he walked off toward the door, the Desk Sergeant returned.

'Sir, could I have a look at those photos, please? Something is hovering at the edge of my memory.'

Bernstein nodded, 'Sure, Sergeant, go ahead.' He spread the photographs out again.'

The Sergeant tapped their man Osier, 'This the man Tasker picked?'

Bernstein nodded, 'It is, yes. You know him?'

'Know is a bit strong, but he used to be a regular drunk tank customer himself. Lemme go look at our registers and get you a name.'

Bernstein realised his hand was trembling slightly in anticipation of a positive result. When the Sergeant came back, Bernstein raised his eyebrows.

'Did you find him?'

The Sergeant nodded, 'Sure did. In this register, the earliest I have, he seems to be recorded three times. Two of them say Kurt Halsted, but the first says John Keller.

Someone has put a line through that and written 'False name, identified as Kurt Halsted' It sure looks convincing to me! Oh, and he hasn't used our hospitality for at least six months. He's either dried out, or drinks in another county!'

Bernstein smiled as he wrote the name.

'Thank you Sergeant, I think you've saved me a ton of time. Thank god for sharp Police Officers. If you ever want to transfer to the FBI, just call me.'

Grinning as he closed his book, the Sergeant said, 'Thank you, sir, but I'm far too fond of the little hill where I live. No wandering all over the country for me, I'm afraid. I'll go see the Chief and ask him if someone can search the records for any convictions, if so, we'll let you know.'

'Thanks again Sergeant,' Bernstein called over his shoulder as he walked out of the door.

As Bernstein entered the FBI field office, young Will Jackson stood from his desk, 'I have a message for you, sir.' He offered a folded piece of paper.

Flipping it open, Bernstein read Halsted's name and home address, the name of the bar where he had been arrested most frequently, and the name of his employer.

'Thanks, Will.'

Bernstein turned and went to see Jim Sullivan in his office. He tapped and poked his head around the door as Jim waved him in.

'Jim, things are moving on quickly now. Will just gave me

our potential suspect's work and home addresses. I'm going to collect McDonald and visit Halsted's home address, any chance I can borrow young Will to go with us, and maybe a car?'

'Sure thing, Will's been itching to get into this!'

'Thanks!' said Bernstein as he closed the door. 'Special Agent Jackson, would you collect a car and meet me outside my office in twenty minutes, please? You know where it is.'

Jackson was already getting to his feet and reaching for his hat.

Bernstein strode out and reached the office quickly. With a wave to Gloria on the landing, he pushed their door open.

'I have news,' he said, as McDonald turned toward him. 'Good or bad?'

'How about Osier's name, address, and workplace?'

McDonald thumped the table, 'Outstanding, Eli!'

Bernstein grinned, 'Grab your coat my friend, we'll go meet our Nazi!'

They parked the car outside a grubby engineering shop on the waterfront. It was the sort of place where spare parts and secondhand equipment are strewn in no identifiable order. Yet the machine shop equipment inside the large triple doors looked well maintained and was all in use. It was the sort of place that can be found in most harbours or waterfronts and can often achieve incredible feats of engineering, whatever their appearance from outside.

Bernstein, McDonald, and Jackson followed the owner up an open mesh stairway, feet clanking on the rungs, the wall in front of them lit by the blue white flash from welding in the shop below.

The owner slid across a payroll information card, which confirmed Halsted's home address. Bernstein noted no next of kin details.

'Thing is fella's, he ain't turned in for work yesterday and today. Didn't call in sick neither. I was going to call round on my way home tonight, but I'm guessing you boys will beat me to it.'

Berstein smiled, 'You're right about that, sir. Before we let you get back to your work, could you tell us what kind of man he is?'

'Sure. He's tough, that's for sure. While he's good at his work he is often a little tardy, but makes up the time at the end of the day. I have to say, he's a drinker. That's what causes him to be late. Most times, he gets on with everyone here, but he gets kinda high and mighty on whether we should remain neutral in the war in Europe. I'm guessing he's from German stock. We just ignore it though, most men have their beliefs.'

Bernstein stood, 'Thank you, sir. We won't take up more of your time, and you've been very helpful.'

'No problem, tell him to give me a call when he can.'

'Will do, sir. Goodbye.'

'So long, take care on the stairway.'

When they were in the car, Berstein adjusted the mirror and caught McDonald's eye in the back seat. He smiled,

'Well that was interesting huh?'

They stepped out of the car as a shower passed over. Leaves whirled and the wet pavement briefly reflected the brickwork of the building in front of them. Standing on William Street, in the Oakdale neighbourhood of Portland, they looked warily at the building in front. It was an old house, but retained some elegance, which was spoiled by dirty shutters and an impressive mound of wet leaves on the front porch.

Bernstein sent Jackson around the back, then knocked firmly on the door. The sound seemed to echo inside, and Bernstein drew his pistol from inside his coat. He was considering whether a forced entry was justified when Jackson appeared around the corner.

'Sir, the yard door has been forced. Nobody in sight in the kitchen.'

Bernstein sucked his teeth for a second, 'You watch here, Will. We'll go around back and Captain McDonald and I will sweep the ground floor.'

Noting the splintered wood of the door frame, they walked in quietly. The house was cold, as was the stove, and there was no sound to be heard. Bernstein knew the house was empty, but was cautious nonetheless. They walked slowly through the ground floor, Bernstein's gun in his hand. At the front door, Bernstein noted the key still in the lock, and quietly opened the door to allow Jackson in. McDonald had stayed behind, looking for any signs of a cellar beneath the building. While he searched, the two agents searched upstairs, returning after finding nothing.

McDonald stood in the hallway and, with a finger to his lips to call for silence, he motioned into a cupboard space beneath the stairway. There was a hatchway in the floor, and a pull-cord for a light hanging from the ceiling of the cupboard. Bernstein stood in front of the hatch and pointed for Jackson to pull the cord. As light spilled from the irregular edges of the hatchway door, he yanked it up and went quickly down the wooden stairway beneath. McDonald heard a muffled, 'All clear guys.' Jackson guarded in the hallway in case anyone returned, and McDonald followed Bernstein into the basement.

At the bottom of the stairs was a basement with a dolly tub washer and mangle. As he turned, McDonald's eyes opened wide. There was one naked lightbulb hanging from the centre of the ceiling, on the far wall was an old leather inlaid desk, complete with bankers lamp and a plush office chair. On the wall was hung a Nazi flag and there were posters for the German-American Bund on either side of it. One poster garishly portrayed the words, 'Wake Up America!' the other was for a 'Pro-American Rally' from 1939.

Bernstein had just picked up a German language copy of Mein Kampf from the desk. McDonald's eye was drawn to some paper in a waste bin. Some sheets were torn but he laid them out on the desk. There were settled bills, two with late payment fees added, and a letter from the tax office rejecting a rebate; just the detritus of a working household. The last two were more interesting by far. One was a letter saying the German-American Bund was sorry he had chosen to cancel his membership, the other was a tenancy agreement for an apartment on Deering Street.

Bernstein explained that this was an area of large properties not far from the downtown area, 'I guess they must've subdivided one of those big houses into apartments,' he explained.

McDonald tutted to himself, 'Do you know what I see here, Eli? I think this is a man who has very carefully organised himself to go dark. He has cut off ties to any organisation that reveals his beliefs, and, looking at the tenancy agreement, may have been establishing a new identity?'

Bernstein considered, 'I agree about hiding his real beliefs, 'but why take on an apartment before he sells up this house? I would expect to see a realtors sign outside the door. No, I think our man has taken an apartment for someone else, if you get my meaning?'

McDonald nodded, 'It fits. All of it fits. His decision to stop drinking, paying off debts, and as we both noticed, leaving the pro-Nazi organisation.'

Bernstein frowned, 'I think we might profitably visit Deering Street, Horace. What do you say?'

Bernstein asked Jackson to stay behind and preserve the scene. His mind had moved into building a case which would stand up in court. He took the wheel and he and McDonald headed for Deering Street.'

Fifteen minutes later, they stood outside a two story wooden clad house. The shower had blown over and the neighbourhood seemed pleasant. The upper story apartment, reached by wooden stairs which were clearly recently built onto the side of the house, was obviously empty. Its uncurtained windows revealed light fittings with no bulbs inserted. Bernstein signed McDonald to check around the back and knocked on the door. Again, there was no answer. McDonald used the radio in the car to ask the field office to despatch a police car to their location as they may need to effect entry. He also asked them to back up Jackson on William Street, he reasoned their quarry might go back there if he wasn't here.

As he returned to the front door, an elderly gentleman appeared on the porch next door, 'Can I help you, sir?'

Bernstein walked over to his house and presented his badge and ID card. A brief talk revealed that the man had a key for the apartment, The owner was sending prospective tenants over and wanted his old neighbour to have a key in case he was engaged elsewhere. He limped off to get the key.

When the old man shuffled back, Berstein smiled at him, 'Thank you sir, I shall return the key as soon as we've checked the apartment. I don't suppose you've spoken to the new tenant?'

'I tried, son, I really did, but the dark-haired guy is plain miserable and the big feller who visits, well, he ain't my kind of person, if you get my drift.'

The hairs stood up on the back of Bernstein's neck. He advised the old man to go inside and returned to his car radio. After requesting the call for police support to be upgraded to urgent, he returned to the door of the apartment. He called to McDonald to join him, remembering the Englishman was unarmed.

At the door, he took out his gun once again, and waved McDonald behind him. Slowly, he turned the key in the door and pushed it silently open. They entered a pleasantly furnished and clean lounge area with a leather upholstered sofa and a Philco radio on a small table. The simply designed fireplace was imposing for the size of the room. McDonald picked up a poker from the fire stand and followed Bernstein through double glass doors. As soon as the doors opened, they smelled death.

Nose crinkling, Bernstein walked further into the room. Sitting on the floor, back against the chair, and slumped slightly sideways, was Kurt Halsted.

There was little blood, and McDonald inspected the dark, bloodstained rip in Halsted's shirt. It looked professional to his eye: between the third and fourth ribs, and, as he recalled from his training, angled slightly upward.

They quartered the whole place, using handkerchiefs to open cupboards and doors, but the place was sterile. The coroner's people would confirm, but it looked like he had wiped away all fingerprints.

Hearing the sirens outside, they left by the front door, being careful to avoid touching objects on their way.

Bernstein briefed the Police Officers, warning them to touch nothing. He also warned the neighbour the police would keep the keys because the apartment was now a crime scene. One detective asked for their fingerprints for elimination, and they agreed to drop by the department on their way back. They handed over the scene and keys to the detectives and, after picking up Jackson and dropping the car at the FBI field office, they returned to their own office for a council of war.

After making fresh coffee, Bernstein sat on the opposite side of McDonald's desk. He'd called Halsted's boss while the coffee brewed, and took a sip of his own before speaking, 'Well, Horace, we know that our friend Willow is one slippery bastard, I guess.'

'I can't disagree, Eli. I wish I could. But you know, we're not as badly off as we were, surely? I mean, we now know the who, and why, we just need to round up where. Now, I had a thought about that. If S.S. Posadilla suddenly leaves, then we are done, because it means that Willow found another way to get the magnetron out of the United States, or Portland, anyway. If she continues to wait, then Willow is still in Portland.'

Bernstein considered for a while, 'Yes, you're right. If he had handed the item to a crew member, they would leave straight away. Ditto if he had abandoned using the ship. Why do I feel we should've already thought of that.'

'Yes, I thought the same thing. Now, what can we do to locate Willow, or flush him from hiding?'

Bernstein rolled his eyes, 'You've reminded me. When I dropped the car back at the field office, I asked them to get the forensic people out of the apartment as quickly as possible and to re-assign manpower if necessary, to maintain a watch on both the house and the apartment. I told them to concentrate manpower on the house, I can't imagine he'd want to go back to the scene of a murder.'

McDonald smiled, 'We've been back footed, Eli, but we're not out of the game.'

'Listen to the guy who has now become the positive one out of the pair!'

'Oh well, I'm not so sure about that, but I do think that we've been making steady progress for a while, plodding if you will, but the pace has picked up in the last day or so, and this must give us a better chance of pressurising Willow into a mistake. The only other thing I thought of was to do a door-to-door survey of the immediate areas of the house and the apartment. You never know what neighbours have spotted, which might seem more significant, if they knew what had happened.'

'Yeah, it did cross my mind whether to do the unthinkable and go public with this. We would have to use the police department, of course. We don't want to tip Willow's hand that you and I are involved. The FBI have had excellent results from enlisting the public over the years, but it feels like firing a musket: it would take too long to reload for another shot if we did that.'

McDonald grimaced, 'Quite. I shudder to think what Sir Peter would say to that! Listen, it's been a long day, what say we find a bar with a decent whisky? That ought to help the thinking process somewhat!

Chapter Fifteen

43° 39' 29" N, 70° 15' 30" W

Portland, Maine

Next morning, McDonald answered his telephone to hear Sir Peter at the other end.

'Hello, sir. It's good to hear your voice, I was going to call you today, as a matter of fact.'

'Oh, splendid. You go first, Horace.'

McDonald gave a blow by blow account of the previous day's events and described his rationale for believing that Willow was still struggling to leave. The issue must be with the network's organisation or resources, he felt, because such a resourceful operator would certainly have solved any problems if they were purely local. He tried to be as upbeat as possible; he knew that Sir Peter would be under an immense amount of pressure from Whitehall until this issue went away. It clearly impressed Sir Peter, he mentioned that his report would be a good deal more interesting today that it had been previously, and he fully intended to make sure his audience knew that this constituted a move toward the endgame, so long as nothing else changed.

There was an extended silence when Sir Peter finished speaking, and when he did start to give McDonald some detail, it was clearly with some embarrassment.

'Well, you see, the thing is that the political classes are working themselves into something of a frenzy about this. The news you've given me today should be enough to keep them quiet for a couple of days, but we need to be prepared for some pressure to use the British Security Coordination team if things don't progress. Now, I assume the FBI would be perfectly happy with that, after all, I think you've already got one man from the BSC with you at the moment, is that right?'

McDonald grimaced, 'That's correct, sir. Just the one.'

'Alright, you know that I'll do anything I can to support you from this end, I'm absolutely confident that you can wrap it up with no help. I'll fight your corner as much as I can and, as I say, we should have a small amount of grace period before they wade in again. So I'll say goodbye now, Dear Boy, and the very best of luck.'

'Thank you, sir. Goodbye.'

He shook his head: he needed coffee.

He'd relayed the conversation to Eli when his telephone rang. It was Gloria informing him that a lady was here to see him. He asked Gloria to show her in, and was delighted to see the young woman who had manned the desk at the BSC in New York when he visited.

'Hello my dear, I'm so sorry, I don't know your full name, but your Christian name is Janet, is it not?'

She smiled, and it went all the way to her eyes, 'Thank you for remembering, sir. For the record, it's Janet Hopkins.' Her eyes swivelled toward Bernstein, who noticed her glance.

'No problem Janet, I was just going to freshen up our coffee pot, anyway. I'll powder my nose while I'm gone.'

Janet smiled as the door closed, 'He's a gentleman, well you both are to be truthful. Now I'll be brief, sir. You are aware of the origin of this message, but just so you know the score, they have disguised it to sound like it came from an agent rather than the process which really produced it, if you get my meaning.'

'Absolutely, Janet, not a problem at all, as I understand it this is common practice. In fact, I'm not sure if they don't have one or two of our chaps there doing the disguising!'

Janet smiled, her hand briefly touching his, 'There was one other thing, sir, whatever my boss says, I think we need to be grateful to you for ridding our office of such an awful man. I shall say no more, but you know who and what I mean. The entire office is grateful.'

McDonald looked into her eyes and knew that he would remember them for some time. He said, 'Thank you, Janet, but really, they had made the decision before I got involved, at least that's what I've been told.'

The door opened and Bernstein appeared with fresh coffee. McDonald waved toward a chair at the side of his desk, 'Do you have a seat, Janet. You'll find the coffee is quite delicious even if the company is lacking.'

Janet laughed as she sat down, then sipped her coffee, making small talk with Bernstein, allowing McDonald to read the transcribed signal.

SIS/ZIP/ZTNG/4663923

FROM: HQ LDN - MOST SECRET

RECEIVED FR AGENT ALPHA THREE THIS DAY. SIGNAL REGARDS EMBEDDED OPERATIVE UNITED STATES.

READS:

U-BOAT FAILED ENTER NEUTRALITY EXCLUSION ZONE STOP HOLD POSITION, AWAIT ONE FURTHER ATTEMPT BEFORE USE OF ORIGINAL ARRANGEMENT STOP NO FURTHER COMMS UNLESS EMERGENCY STOP.

DESTROY WHEN READ: MOST SECRET

McDonald suppressed a slight smile: Bernstein would recognise a smokescreen when he saw it. If he knew about the US Navy rebuffing the offer of intelligence sharing, then he'd be very aware that Station X at Bletchley Park had people who hid their decryption by adding details of imaginary informants or double agents. He'd also know this was good information.

He chatted with Janet until she finished her coffee. As she

stood, McDonald couldn't believe his own ears, when he said, 'Do you have a telephone number that I can reach you on, Janet? Just in case I need to follow up, you understand.'

Janet blushed in the most charming way, and, turning over a page in his notebook, which was on the desk, scribbled inside. She quickly turned to leave, calling goodbye over her shoulder, but not making eye contact with Bernstein.

Bernstein spluttered with laughter, 'Hell, Horace, you are some mover.'

McDonald reddened in his turn, then turned to ash as he read the words on his notebook page, the message simply said, 'Not on your life'.

Laughing despite himself, McDonald closed the notebook. Glancing up, he said, 'You'd better come and look at this, Eli. I think it will make your day.'

He pushed the 'transcription' over his desk.

Sipping his coffee as Bernstein read the slip of paper, McDonald could feel the relief washing through him. He didn't like the 'one more attempt' comment, but knew he had a deterrent if the Skipper were at sea.

The Skipper and Number One were discussing ways to keep the lads busy and didn't notice that McDonald had come on board until he appeared in the wheelhouse.

'Hello chaps,' beamed McDonald, 'Don't worry, your people did challenge me but recognised me and allowed me up.'

The Skipper put down his deck log, 'Good morning, sir. Grand to see you.'

'And you, Skipper. Do you have a few minutes to talk? It is rather urgent, but five minutes won't hurt.'

'No problem, sir, we were just about finished. Trying to keep the boys busy!'

McDonald's eyes crinkled, 'I may be able to help you with that issue, Skipper. We could have a problem with a U-boat attempting to pick up one of our targets in Casco Bay. I'm afraid I'm going to have to ask you to resume your patrolling. Your cover story will be that you're on an exercise with the United States Coast Guard, and I must ask you to get out there as quickly as you can.'

The Skipper grabbed the intercom, 'Archie, can you begin raising steam please?'

'No problem, Skipper.'

Archie, the second engineer, began the process. He called for the fireman, Danny Irton, and asked him to get ready. Raising steam was an easier and quicker job when not done from cold. Danny used an iron tool called a slice bar to remove some clinker from between the bars of the grating in the starboard fire box, he then opened the damper, and re-distributed the coals with his firing hoe into a heap, adding more coal and opening the draught plate. When it burned up, he would redistribute it into a thin flat layer across the grating to ensure that the boiler was efficient, and not producing smoke. Once he'd done that he began repeating the process in the port fire box. They'd found that having one side hot first caused convection in the water and spread the heat more effectively.

While this was going on, Archie was opening drains to purge the pipe between the boiler and the engine of any liquid water, which could in no circumstances be allowed to enter the engine. He used litmus paper to check the feed water and a hydrometer to check its density. The feedwater could not be acidic, had to be pure, and contain no salt water. This was precautionary because they had been static for a while. He then began easing various valves off their seats slightly. This would prevent them jamming when they heated up. The steam valves were already slightly open to warm the engine. He checked the boiler water level, made sure that cylinder and slide-chest drains were open to the bilge, this was to check for oil or grease as they made steam. He checked the auxiliary machinery, the stern gland greaser and the pumps.

Svein appeared at the bottom of the ladder, and grinned at Archie, 'We're getting underway, eh?'

Archie gave him a thumbs up 'Would you blow down the gauge glass as we get some steam pressure? I'll shake up another fireman to help Daniel adjust the draught plates once the boiler's in trim. They can move some coal down too.'

'Yah, no problem there. I'll lift the safety valves once we get some pressure. Then you can let the engine have some steam once it's ready.' He checked the boiler feed pump steam valve to make sure it was slightly open, he'd open it fully when the pressure rose so the boiler was getting the right input of feedwater. He made doubly sure the boiler water glass gauge tube was clean and they could easily make out the level. After a quick look around, he pronounced himself satisfied with the preparations.

Back in the wheelhouse, McDonald explained that they could only function as a deterrent, they could not attack a contact, however; they were at liberty to report it to a United States destroyer, which would be on hand in the northeast of Casco Bay. The U.S. ship would be patrolling in the deep waters outside, as they had recently done, so White Nab could concentrate on the waters between the islands with her slightly shallower draught. In dire straits, an 'accidental collision' or running the u-boat aground somehow would be acceptable, just.

As they would be working inshore, the Skipper decided the two lads currently in the observation post could stay there if they could be provided with food and drink. Number One confirmed they were being fed, mostly cold food, but every other day they went out for a warm meal in a diner once they had finished their hitch.

'We'll cope sir, especially as we won't need the gun crew, sad though that may be,' his eyes twinkled as he spoke, turning toward McDonald.

'Well, you could throw something at them, if it helps Skipper?'

'Not really, sir, no.'

Billy had brought tea, 'Here you go gentlemen, gulp it down sharp, sir, you don't want to get left on board when we sail!' He smiled at McDonald.

'No fear Billy, I've been practising the Skipper's pier head jump!'

As they finished their tea, the intercom buzzer sounded. The Skipper pressed the toggle.

'Now then, Archie, has the boiler gone up?'

'It's Svein, Skipper, and it's worse than that, we'll have steam up in about an hour, maybe less, and Billy was going to cook me a slap up meal this evening!'

'Patience is a virtue, Svein.'

'Well, yah, but salt cod sounded pretty damn fine!'

There was a pause, 'Fair enough Svein, if you like that sort of thing. Thanks for the news though, I'll get Arthur to give the deck hands a prod shortly.'

McDonald drained his cup and reminded them of the frequency for contacting Eli's men in Boston if needed.

'Thanks, sir. I'll start at the outside and establish contact with the destroyer, then work my way as far inshore as I can. We'll have a reasonable expectation that the area is clear once we've done that.'

'Thanks, Skipper,' McDonald waved as he turned to go down the ladder to the deckhouse roof.

When the steam pressure had risen, the vents all showed steam and were closed. They opened the steam valve a little more, just enough to introduce steam pressure to bring the engine and auxiliary equipment to working temperature. Finally, they checked for leaks, moved the engine slowly, ahead and astern, then Svein buzzed the Skipper.

'Ready for sea Skipper.'

'Thanks, Svein. I'll try my best to swing a salt cod break for you.'

'Yah, maybe better we fuel her on wood. We could smoke herring in the funnel. Nice side-line, eh?'

'You're as daft as I am Svein!'

The Skipper nodded to Arthur, who went down on deck with his oilskins on. The rain was bouncing back off the deck. Somehow, he had acquired six waxed cap-covers for the ship's officers, but then decided the water went down his neck and had reverted to his trusty sou'wester.

They left half an hour before high water, so the Skipper decided he would cut between the two Diamond Islands and Peaks Island, via Diamond Island Pass. The harbour master had warned that there was a good deal of activity to the west of Great Diamond Island because of army training, and this narrower cut would give him a feel for navigation in Casco Bay.

Once through, and into Hussey Sound, he turned south-easterly to pass between Peaks Island and the southern side of Long Island. The rain had eased, and he could see low-lying, pleasantly wooded islands, both port and starboard.

Once out of the shower, and he turned south-southeast to enter the deeper water and begin searching for the destroyer. As the Skipper scanned the horizon over to port, he noticed a whale, possibly a humpback, just breaking surface. In the sound, he had also seen two porpoises tracking alongside for a while. As the afternoon watch entered its last hour, the lookout reported a warship to the north-east. The Skipper waited for 20 minutes before they could clearly identify her as a destroyer: USS Leary, DD-158. She was a first war vintage four-stacker, but still looked proud, with her number painted large near the bow, and a white bone in her teeth. He asked Pickering to identify White Nab to her, and to inform Leary they would begin the inshore patrol immediately. Leary acknowledged, and White Nab turned for the Broad Sound channel where the Skipper planned to turn southwest between Bang and Stave Islands, before turning back south of Hope Island and heading up Luckse Sound. They did everything at a snail's pace, but the Skipper was gaining confidence in the charts, which were proving accurate.

As dusk stole upon them, they were east of Bustins Island and planned to pass around the northern coast of Upper Goose Island before circling Middle Bay. In these shallow waters, the ASDIC was next to useless, but they pinged intermittently as a deterrent if the water depth exceeded 45 feet. In between pings, they left the ASDIC in passive mode, with Yorke and Pickering spelling each other, listening for propellor or compressed air noises which might reveal a u-boat. Number One had suggested that the sub skipper might lie doggo on the bottom, waiting for an extraction after nightfall.

For the next two days, White Nab patrolled Casco Bay, to no avail. There was a moment's excitement at dusk on the middle evening. A white wake sliced across from starboard bow to port. The lookouts immediately suspected a periscope and turned on the searchlight, to reveal a dolphin or small whale's dorsal fin cutting through the water. The weather had been changeable, but in the better periods, the Skipper decided he liked this place. He sensed there would be fish offshore, and of course the Grand Banks, off the coast of Newfoundland, were legendary.

Halfway through the forenoon watch, they were between Outer Green Island and The Hussey. Arthur had the bridge while the Skipper was looking at the tidal flows and rise of tide graphs.

Suddenly, Nev Danby squawked from within the W/T office, 'Can you fix a position please Arthur? I'm on a really powerful signal.' Nev had been monitoring the channels that Nazi spies had used in the past.

The Skipper looked up, 'I'll get that Arthur, you just make sure we're clear of that buoy south of the shoal.'

Once he had plotted their position from a couple of bearings, with an extra one for confirmation, he noted the latitude and longitude, and joined Neville in the wireless office.

Nev turned as the Skipper entered, 'I just had a signal from the Boston intercept site, once they have our position and the bearing to the signal, they'll reply with our man's location almost immediately. Hopefully, we'll get a decent fix on this one, Skipper.' The Skipper slapped the position on Nev's table and crossed his fingers as Nev began tapping his morse key.

The Skipper was about to go back into the wheelhouse when the staccato pattern of Morse code could be heard coming from Nev's earphones. Nev's finger was raised, as he jotted on a signal pad with his other hand: his grin said it all.

'Here you go, Skipper, that's his location, according to Mr Bernstein's Boston colleagues. Nearly instant!'

Dashing for the chart table, the skipper picked up his plotter and a soft pencil. When he had marked the position on his chart, his eyebrows knitted together.

'According to this, he's in the middle of Broad Cove!'

He quickly laid off the route, following the deepest water available so he could go as fast as possible. He rang for full ahead, and they built up speed as they turned to head southwest until they could turn to clear the Hussey, marked as rock on the Skipper's chart. They then turned northwest to pass between Peaks and Long Islands, coming round to due north to pass just east of Cow Island. Using transits, he passed between Sturdivant and Basket Islands, being careful to avoid the upper Clapboard Ledge. He kept to the east of Sturdivant Island, with the idea that he'd be more central in the bay and able to react which ever direction the Nazi took. By this point, everybody realised he must be in a boat, and that was why searches on land had failed.

The Skipper frowned, 'Arthur, I'll take the watch, can you get a few of the lads and ready both boats please? Maybe get one ready to go over the rail as soon as we spot our man.'

'Will do Skipper, I'll leave it hanging on the falls so we can get the lads into it before we lower away.'

As Arthur left, the Skipper buzzed the flying bridge and explained that he wanted the bearings to any boats visible to the northwest after they rounded Sturdivant Island, with one lookout monitoring each boat if possible. They needed clues on which boat to challenge and board. As he cleared Sturdivant Island Broad Cove opened up and he steered northwest to stay in the deepest water.

In the event, there was no need for any clues as to their quarry. On rounding the northern tip of the island. Broad Cove opened up to their view and only three boats were visible within the cove. Two of them were fishing, but the third, a motor launch, was travelling at some speed toward Anderson Rock. The Skipper quickly consulted the chart and shouted down to Number One, who was in the ship's well with some deckhands, asking him to get someone in the chains with the lead line. He knew he would need to get as close as possible, without running aground, before he got the boat away. He noticed on the chart that there was a steep shelving of the bottom about 1 ½ cables from shore, so he worked out a bearing on a prominent building so he knew when to drop the hook. The launch had passed Anderson's Rock, and the Skipper could now make out a small jetty to the south of it. He adjusted course, recalculated his bearing, and, stepping out onto the bridge wing, he called down to Number One to shout up him when they got into three fathoms. The launch would get there first, so the Skipper reduced speed and warned Svein that he might need full astern at very short notice. A couple of minutes later, Number One shouted, and gave him a thumbs up, so the

Skipper rang full astern and called down to Arthur, near the boat, to get it away. As he shouted, Number One sprinted down the deck, then pointed to the boat, eyebrows raised. The Skipper yelled, telling him to get into the boat, and do his best to stop the man.

Back inside the wheelhouse, he yanked open the wireless room door and asked Neville if he could raise Bernstein's men in Boston. He was to ask if they could call Bernstein and tell him to get men to the jetty, south of Anderson Rock in Broad Cove, where their target was fleeing. Arthur, now back in the wheelhouse, called through.

'Skipper, the boat has now run ashore and I can see steps going up from the rocks or beach. Our lads are close, but he will have a head start on them. They might still pincer him if they look sharp.'

Nev glanced up and nodded. It only took two or three minutes and he popped his head out of his kennel, as their other watch-keeper, Fred, liked to call it.

'They're on their way Skipper. Apparently, the road's called Town Landing, so they're flooding the area with manpower.'

The Skipper thumped the coaming, 'This might be it, lads!'

'Signal, Skipper. We are to return to Portland but berth forward of the Spanish ship as soon as the FBI agents release the lads who are onshore.'

'Thanks, Nev. Acknowledge that please,' he glanced around the bridge, grinning, 'Looks like we'll be blockading now!'

Number One carefully watched the sparsely wooded slope in front of them as the lads stowed their oars and heaved the forefoot of the boat up above the waterline. Rolling a heavy rock on to the painter, the boat was secure. Number One was genuinely impressed by the speed with which George Sneaton had tied a monkey's fist knot on the end of the painter.

Seeing nothing to cause alarm, they first looked at the motor launch, which had struck hard and badly damaged the bow. Number one asked George to check the launch and pocket any papers or move equipment that shouldn't be onboard above the tide-line, then join them uphill. He had a man on either side on the cut heading uphill. The trees were mostly bare on this seaward slope, but there were a few leaves which clung on to their parent.

Number One, his jaw set, asked the lads to look for any sign their man might have cut off parallel to the shore. He himself kept watch up-slope as they made gradual progress toward the top of the rise. There was nothing to be seen, no scuffs at the side of the track, no disturbed leaves.

Number One froze as a swarthy, dark-haired man appeared, coming down the hill. Realising that he was wearing a dark suit, it was clear he was not their man. An opinion which was confirmed when he raised a badge and called, 'FBI!'

Number One identified himself, then quickly briefed the

agent on what they had seen. As he spoke, Sneaton came jogging up the hill.

'Nothing in the launch sir, I'm wondering if he ditched his transmitter overboard.'

'It's likely, George. Well done.'

Hearing sirens uphill, the FBI man turned, calling over his shoulder.

'I'd better get back guys, the police will be here with dogs soon. Thanks for the tip-off.'

The man dashed off, uphill.

Number One turned, 'We'll go back to the ship lads, otherwise people might wonder why a party of British sailors appear to have invaded! Well done to you all. I must say, I felt a bit exposed being unarmed, but hopefully we kept our man off balance. It's up to the FBI and police now.'

Bernstein and McDonald tumbled out of their car. They could see Jim Sullivan directing both police and FBI, and the sound of dogs echoed in the trees. Seeing that everything was in hand, Bernstein suggested they take a drive to cruise any streets that Willow might use to get back toward Halsted's house.

For thirty minutes, they cruised around, to no avail. They had one false alarm who turned out to be a salesman but drew a blank and eventually decided to return to Sullivan's location for an update.

They found Sullivan doing house to house enquiries at

the top of the hill. As he turned away from a gentleman in dungarees holding a machine part, he shook his head.

'Nothing Gentlemen, I'm afraid. I'm thinking he had an exit strategy long planned. I've assigned more men to watch the house, mainly intermittent drive-bys so as not to alert him, but he's going to be real twitchy now...'

Bernstein pursed his lips, 'How about the dogs?'

'Still finishing their search routine on the south side, we did that first because it's the most likely direction. Then they'll do the north. In fact, here they come now.'

As they looked downhill, they could see the handlers crossing the road. Two of the dogs suddenly stopped and went rigid, pointing uphill. The handler followed them, giving encouragement as he ran with the dogs. Occasionally, they would lose the scent, but pick it up again in a few paces.

They followed the team uphill and watched. At the roadside, the dogs seemed to lose the scent again. The handlers crossed and tried to pick it up. Just as they were ready to stop, the lead dog pointed again. He strained against the leash and pulled away up Tuttle Road. They all grinned with relief, but two hundred yards later the dog lost scent again and, no matter how far they went northwest, they couldn't find it again.

Bernstein grimaced, 'Someone picked the bastard up Horace, he's in the breeze again!'

McDonald's head bowed as they trudged back to inform Sullivan. He felt like a boxer on the ropes, hanging on, but losing. It felt further going back than it had coming uphill.

Chapter Sixteen

43° 39' 29" N, 70° 15' 30"

Portland, Maine

After crossing the road, they spotted Sullivan walking toward them. Bernstein waved, 'We lost him Jim, he's on the lam again!'

Sullivan walked up, looking serious, 'Things might not be as bad as you think, Boss. See, they just had a walk in at the field office, and called me on the radio. It seems an old guy who lives in Portland picked someone up near Cumberland, but may know where he'll be later. I guess you'll want to speak with him?'

McDonald looked shellshocked, while Bernstein gave a triumphant grin.

'Well Horace, we were due for a lucky break. Thanks to the Skipper, we may have been in the right place to get it!

They ran to the car, and fifteen minutes later, they were

in the FBI office, speaking to an elderly gentleman who looked slightly flustered.

'As I already told the other agent, I walk my dog in the evening and as I leave my apartment I can see across to the windows of the diner on Newbury Street from my stair landing. It's an Italian place, I think. Anyhow, nearly every night, I see this guy through the window, kinda mean looking, menacing, if you know what I mean. His appearance caught my attention and because I'm on my own now, I often make up stories to amuse myself. This guy is a gangster in my imagination, but in real life, who knows? He might be a good samaritan. At least that's what I thought until today. So, I'm driving back from doing some errands in Cumberland, and who do I see standing at the side of the road, but my gangster! So, thinking that charity begins at home, I pull over and ask him if he needs a ride. Now, I didn't want him thinking that I'm weird, so I didn't tell him I'd seen his face before. I just acted like I'd picked him up because it's a long road. Anyhow, I ask him where he needs dropping, and he said he'd like to get out anywhere on the waterfront. He said that the Commercial and Park Street junction would be ideal. That's it really, except for one thing. As he left my car, the bag he'd had in between his legs, a kind of leather haversack, well, it fell open when he pulled the handle. But the strange thing was, inside it looked like he'd got some sort of wireless apparatus. There were earphones and what looked like a Morse key. I realised that was quite odd, so I decided to swing by this office and let you guys know. I mean, there are amateur radio enthusiasts, I know, but taking your gear out in a bag, well, that just seemed a little strange. Then I began thinking of all this talk of Nazi spies, and thought to myself, no sir, let someone else deal with this. If I'm wasting your time, I can only apologise.'

Bernstein had let him get it all out so he could gauge the man's character and he seemed genuine. Eli reassured him he was not wasting their time, and asked if there had been any further conversation, which there had not. With an admonition not to speak of this to anyone, Bernstein let him go, advising him not to walk the same way that evening.

When the boat returned, Number One supervised recovery and stowage of the boat and oars while Arthur picked up the lead line, ready to feel their way out of the shallow water. They had already brought her about and were ready to head off to Portland. They crept slowly back toward Basket Island, turning due east when the Skipper judged there was enough water under the keel to be safe from grounding. He had previously marked up a line on the chart to a building on Cousins Island, and he knew that would get him into the deeper water to head south-southwest. Never comfortable manoeuvering in shoal waters when the tide was on the first of the ebb, he decided to go east of Peaks Island to stay in deeper water.

As evening turned to a wet night, they tied up, bows on to the Spaniard, starboard side to the Long Wharf. Number

One made sure the 4-inch gun was level so that it would remind the Spanish skipper of their capabilities every time he looked out of his wheelhouse.

The Skipper asked Number One to see the FBI agents in the observation post, and to tell them he would run strict harbour watches, so the Spaniard was constantly under observation from White Nab. He assumed this would free up some manpower for them and he'd get his whole crew back.

As the Skipper tidied up his charts and Arthur made sure the wheelhouse was tidy, Svein was chatting to Billy about salt cod.

'It's called bacalao, Billy. I've written the recipe down. Basically, it's a stew of salt cod and potatoes, but with lots of tinned tomatoes and some peppers and garlic. I'm pretty sure you'll get most of the ingredients around here.'

Billy was still reeling about Norwegians eating peppers and garlic.

Arthur was getting a lot of free entertainment from their conversation, but noticed a uniformed customs chap approaching on the wharf. Climbing down to deck level, he welcomed the man onboard. He was FBI in reality and passed on a message asking the Skipper to go to see McDonald at his earliest opportunity. He left a scrap of paper with the address in case the Skipper needed it.

Bernstein whistled as he made coffee. They had grabbed a

hamburger on the way back to the office and Bernstein had booked a table at the late-opening Italian restaurant. He felt the need for lobster, but he suspected they'd be busy later and told them to close up if he didn't show before their usual closing time, and not to wait for him.

'So, what do you say, Horace? It seems we've been lucky; I know the old guy was a bit flaky, but it seems to me everything ties in with his story. When things are too neat, it usually makes me suspicious, but in this case, I think it's the real deal.'

McDonald sipped and put down his cup, 'I couldn't agree more, Eli. I'm also thinking back to the signal we had from England. I assumed that the original arrangements which it mentions meant boarding the Spanish freighter, or trusting the Spanish captain with the magnetron. Now I'm wondering if there is a wider picture. Maybe Willow has been using the café as a meeting place. Perhaps he's running his network from there, or possibly waiting for a contact to appear. If it's the latter, I wonder whether we are looking at a wider network already in existence.'

Bernstein nodded, 'All true, but what really matters at the moment, the key factor if you like, is that we have a location where Willow is likely to be. Now, after the events of today, he may be more skittish, but I think it's the best chance we've got for apprehending him. If he has the magnetron with him, all the better, but if he hasn't, and we can capture him alive, that's the best chance you have of retrieving it.'

'Yes, I thought about that. The original arrangement, which was mentioned in the signal, could refer to just about anything, but I still think the most likely explanation is that it refers to the Spanish freighter in someway. Otherwise, what an earth is the Spaniard waiting for?'

Bernstein was about to reply when the door opened, and the Skipper walked in.

'Good evening gentlemen, I'm reporting as requested.'

McDonald beamed, 'Skipper! Good to see you, and extremely well done today. We'll fill you in shortly but I want to say, yourself and your crew may well have opened up the investigation to where we may make an arrest and recover the missing item.'

'That's good news, sir. Can I help in any way?'

'I hope so, Skipper. I haven't spoken to Mr Bernstein yet, because we were only just starting to discuss a plan, but I have some thoughts. It's likely that we know where our target will be this evening. Now, we don't have a lot of time, and certainly not enough to plan a major multi-agency operation. So I'm wondering if we could use one of your officers to boost our numbers. The target we seek is a professional in the intelligence game. He will be trained and seems very experienced, so he is highly likely to recognise surveillance. I would suggest that we don't flood the location, which is a café by the way, and the people we do use should, if possible, be non-professionals to minimise the risk of making him suspicious.'

Bernstein nodded, 'I think that's a reasonable suggestion. To be honest, I would say we need either yourself or me, plus one other in the location and a wider net around it for detection or capture, depending on whether he's already there when we arrive. I actually think, Horace, that the Skipper himself would be a good choice.'

The Skipper smiled, 'No problem, sir. Anything I can do to help if it captures a Nazi!'

Bernstein had opened the map on the table, he was smoothing out the folds and running his finger up Newbury Street.

'OK, so the Village Café, as it's called, is near the junction of Newbury and Hancock. Here,' he stabbed his finger on the map, 'we have a cemetery here but the entrance is to the north, however there are the Thomas Laughlin Company buildings on Hancock Street, just around the corner. It's a marine engineering outfit, I think. I'll get my people to see if the owners can let us have access to a building in which to hide until we have our man in sight.' He looked at McDonald with eyebrows raised.

'Yes, I'd say so. Let me propose this plan to you: the Skipper and myself will be in the café, Skipper, I'll pose as a shipping agent and you as a merchant captain, sit facing Willow if possible, on the off chance he caught sight of me today. We can talk about a cranage issue which will delay your departure and you can complain that it risks you having to wait for the next eastbound convoy. If he leaves and walks toward Eli's location we can let them know and wait to block his retreat. If he goes the other way, I'll try to nab him myself with you as backup; once we let Eli know, of course.'

Bernstein nodded, 'Yeah, no problem. One thing though, can't we hide a man or two in the kitchen?

Obviously we couldn't take Willow inside, it might get nasty; but we could have our guys on his back quicker than if they were around the corner.'

McDonald smiled, 'Thanks Eli, but this chap is on a hair trigger, I suspect. He's in survival mode and has got perfect instincts from what we've seen so far. If the waiters or owner changed their behaviour or character even a little, he'll see it and disappear. Again!'

Bernstein laughed, then turned as the door opened. It was Sullivan.

'How's everyone doing?' He looked around the three sitting men.

Bernstein nodded, 'OK, thanks. We've been planning for the apprehension of our Nazi spy. But I think we're going to need your help.'

He explained the plan, and the rationale behind having two people who were not in local law enforcement. Sullivan broke off to call his office and muster some of his best men. Bernstein then filled in the plan's detail inside the café, then he and Sullivan worked out logistics for the FBI contingent. The Skipper asked if he could go to change and suggested he brief his officers to patrol Commercial Street near the wharf as a potential block before the wharf itself. Sullivan said that young Jackson would take him in a car and drop him off, either at the field office or the factory where they would hold a final briefing for participants only, and issue weapons and radios.

Bernstein looked thoughtful, 'Skipper, let's try to keep your crew out of this as much as possible. If this turns into a shooting war, which it might, then we don't want them in the crossfire unarmed. Worse, they might be mistaken for the enemy.'

Will Jackson sped the car down to the Commercial Street, parking out of sight of the Spanish ship to let the Skipper out. He said he'd wait a little further down the road and would turn around before he got back, so they were ready to leave.

Once onboard, the Skipper called Number One and Arthur up to the wheelhouse and filled them in on the details. He explained that, in the unlikely event that Willow escaped, the Nazi would have no other option than the Spanish freighter. Making it clear they were to keep the crew on board for the evening, he asked them to explain the situation to the lads. He said the Spanish crew were unlikely to get involved shore side, but given they had expressed a wish to leave quickly, he suspected they might take things into their own hands if they sensed they might get delayed. Finally, he told Arthur to take an unloaded Lee Enfield up to the wheelhouse so he could threaten the crew, or the spy, with no neutrality issues arising. At least, that's what he hoped.

'Right lads, I'll be off now, time to get a spy into the cod end of the net!'

Chapter Seventeen

43° 39' 29" N, 70° 15' 30"

Portland, Maine

Bernstein called the meeting to order. They were in a large office on a steel mesh mezzanine deck over a machine shop.

'OK, listen in guys. We've had to set this operation up in a hurry, so forgive us for some of the odd arrangements we've had to put in as a necessity. The first of which, and please don't laugh, is the fact that we are using whistles as warning signals.'

As he'd expected, that raised a round of laughter.

'But seriously, every man here will need to be very sharp this evening. We've acquired some coveralls and brown lab coats so that we can vary our appearance, but our intention is to keep the main body of our manpower in this office, with occasional walking patrols to get current information.

We are using our British friends inside the café, because I don't think anyone would mistake them for FBI. When the target leaves the café, Mr McDonald and Skipper Hurton will immediately follow him and give the signal for us to move. If we can then nab him, all to the good, but if not, our British friends will stop and restrain the target so that we can make a formal arrest. As they leave, they will give three loud blasts on the whistle and we will need to get around that corner, real fast. Once the target is confirmed as being inside, we shall be doing walk-bys, but we can't all go out on the street in plain sight, just in case the target is waiting for a contact to meet him in the restaurant. We will have three radio cars, Unit One will be the command car here, Unit Two will be on Hampshire to cover an exit southwest, and Unit Three will be on Mountfort in case he runs northeast. Skipper Hurton has quite a few of sensible guys on his ship, who we'll hold in reserve in case something happens on the waterfront. OK, take a minute to digest that and let me have questions. I'll just run down to the car and do a radio check before things hot up.'

Except for a couple of minor clarifications, there were no questions, and the meeting ended with that dry-mouthed tension most people feel before decisive action.

The Skipper ambled his way up Hancock Street, turning left into Newbury. The Village Cafe sign stuck out of the wall ahead of him, on his side of the road. He felt slightly out of his depth, but knew that he had a lot of support. He smiled to himself when he realised that his primary worry was how he was to string out his meal, if the target didn't arrive quickly.

He ascended the stairs slowly, after leaving his coat on a hook down below, and the waitress led him through the dark, cosy room to the seat at the back which Bernstein had requested, using the excuse they were talking business and didn't need a window view.

Walking across the middle of the room, he saw with horror that Willow had arrived. He sat in a booth in front of their table, slightly off to the left.

As he sat, he realised why this place was described as Portland's most popular place to eat by the local FBI men. It had a fine atmosphere, and he hoped he'd get some food before anything happened. He checked out the drinks menu, ordering a beer and some olives while he waited for his shipping agent. He thought he'd been quite clever getting that in while the place was quiet.

As Bernstein had suggested before he left, he fixed his gaze on the menu and avoided glancing at Willow, but he risked a quick look up when the door opened for a young couple with a child. He could clearly see the scar as Willow leaned forward to look at the door. The Skipper kept to the script, looking down at his own menu.

His drink had arrived, so he took a sip and speared an olive with a cocktail stick. It was all very real now.

Ten minutes passed before McDonald entered the restaurant. He waited behind a middle-aged couple and a family with three very excited children, one of whom seemed to be celebrating her birthday.

Climbing the stairs, he entered the café and spotted the Skipper at the far end. The Skipper half stood and silently waved a hand as if showing someone he was there. McDonald knew this wasn't in the script, so he kept his eyes on the Skipper as he walked down the restaurant.

Approaching the table, the Skipper stood and extended his hand, 'Good evening, Mr McDonald.

'Good evening yourself, Captain Hurton. I trust the cargo has arrived and has been loaded?'

'Ah, well, there is the problem, you see. It appears we've only received half of the cargo. Can you update me on the remaining loads?'

This was the phrase they had agreed just before the Skipper left the factory. 'The full load is onboard' meant two men were present, 'half load' meant one, 'no cargo has arrived' meant that Willow wasn't present.

McDonald cleared his throat, 'Yes, sorry about that. They had some cranage issues at the other end and had to hitch the remaining cargo onto a different train, unfortunately.'

Once they were both seated they lowered their voices, hoping that Willow had heard snatches of what they had just said.

McDonald thought quickly as he looked at the menu. He had expected them to be waiting for Willow to show up, but he wondered if the fact that he was already here and waiting might indicate that he was to be met. He looked up at the

Skipper and spoke with a lowered voice.

'Does he seem on edge Skipper?'

The Skipper leaned forward, 'More watchful than edgy, I'd say. He was here when I arrived, so I've done as Mr Bernstein suggested and kept my eyes off him apart from an occasional glance around the room.'

McDonald nodded, 'Well done. I'm wondering if they have ordered him to wait here for a certain length of time each evening, perhaps in anticipation of meeting someone for further instructions. What I don't understand is where the freighter fits in, why they didn't just get him on board and go.' As he spoke, he realised the most likely explanation was that Willow was a key figure in the emerging network, and that meant he was most likely to be waiting for a courier to arrive to take the magnetron and travel back to Spain on the freighter. Willow must be planning to stay in the United States and continue building the network. It seemed to fit the facts, at least.

The waitress appeared with a menu for McDonald. He asked for the same starter as the Skipper to start, while he looked at the menu. As he spoke, the Skipper saw Willow's head lift and his flinty eyes seemed locked on McDonald.

Chapter Eighteen

43° 39' 29" N, 70° 15' 30"

Portland, Maine

Leaning forward, the Skipper kept his voice very low, 'Sir, I think that our man just recognised your voice. He looked and stared when you spoke.' He had to work hard to avoid glancing over at Willow, but his instincts said there was a steady gaze trained on him.

McDonald considered for a moment, 'I don't recall him being identified as a member of the Nazi intelligence services. So far as we know, they don't know who our individual officers are. That said, they may know who the head of my organisation is and I've appeared in public as his aide, along with my boss, so he may have heard me speak. I don't think it's likely though, perhaps he only just realised I'm English? In any event, I think we need to just stick it out; the next move has to be on him, or whoever may or may not come to meet him.'

The Skipper nodded and speared another olive. McDonald laughed loudly, then winked at the Skipper, 'Relax and smile, it'll put him off balance if he thinks we're unconcerned.'

The Skipper beamed at him and the entry of another customer allowed him an opportunity to quickly glance over. Willow was checking his watch and looking at the door. He smiled again as he told McDonald what he'd seen.

McDonald answered, 'It's coming up on seven o'clock, maybe he has to wait here between six and seven. I'm wondering if he's waiting for a courier to take the item back over the pond. That would explain why the freighter is still here. If that's correct, and I were him, I'd tell the courier that I'll be in a certain location at set times and to meet me when prepared to leave.

The Skipper nodded, thinking that these lads spent a lot of time trying to work out solutions to constantly changing information. He was just about to say as much when he saw movement out of the corner of his eye.

'Willow's on the move, sir,' said the Skipper tensely.

McDonald threw a handful of dollars on the table and stood.

'Leave this for the meal and wait for one minute before you follow me.'

McDonald left without waiting for a reply. The Skipper

checked his watch, then waved to the waitress, pointing to the cash on the table.

He moved over to the stairway and waited a few seconds before dashing down to grab his coat. As he emerged, it was dark, and the streetlights were on. Turning to his left, he went cold. Willow was struggling with McDonald and as the Skipper turned to help, someone hurled him to the floor. Getting up, it horrified him to see Willow plunge a knife into McDonald's chest. Willow was turning and running while the man who had shoved the Skipper over was holding McDonald back, with his hands around his throat. The Skipper lurched forward just as McDonald reached up and pulled the knife from his shoulder, ramming it into his assailant just under the ribcage. The man dropped, motionless, as the Skipper reached McDonald.

'It was only in my shoulder Skipper. Get after him, I'm fine. As if to illustrate his point he blew three loud blasts on his whistle, which were repeated some distance behind them. The Skipper shrugged off his coat and ran. He could still see Willow ahead, but knew that he had a lot of ground to make up.

He decided to sprint so he could close the distance before they were both tired. Willow was still going west on Newbury Street, and the Skipper worked hard to close the distance. He ran straight over the first two junctions, but nearly fell at the Franklin Street crossing as a car swerved to avoid him. He was only around fifty yards behind Willow when suddenly the Nazi swerved left. As the

Skipper reached the narrow cut, a car with sirens on pulled in, its headlights dazzling. The Skipper pointed down the alley without slowing. He thought he heard someone get out, then the car reversed, and he heard the squeak of tyres as it sped off. Hopefully, the FBI chaps would intercept at the next road south. The Skipper fervently hoped so, his lungs were getting painfully raw.

Ahead, he saw Willow angle right as he ran into the light. There was a blaring of horns and the Skipper pressed on at full speed, relying on drivers having stopped as Willow ran across. They had, not least because someone had seemingly piled into the back of another car, which must have braked hard to avoid Willow. Following the angle Willow had taken, the Skipper entered Deer Street, with Willow only about forty yards ahead. He hoped he could keep gaining, but was aware he was tiring. He prayed Willow was tiring more, or that a younger and fitter FBI man took over at some point!

Onboard White Nab, Arthur watched as a few of the crew wandered down on to the wharf. It looked like some of the Spanish crew were gathering further down. Billy came crashing into the wheelhouse, his eyes darting between Fred and Arthur.

'The Spaniards are trying to block off the wharf, Arthur. I just got shoved back, and I was only going to see if I could get some milk from somewhere, ours has gone off a bit.'

Number One had come in, 'Looks like trouble chaps. I'll go down.'

Fred grinned, 'Don't trouble yourself sir, this is just Hull docks on a Saturday evening. Our lads can handle themselves, but with my help, if you'll permit me?'

Number One grinned, 'I shall be right there with you, Mister Braithwaite. Shall we go?'

Fred rubbed his beefy hands together, 'Let me lead, sir. I suspect brawling on the dockside would be frowned upon for a commissioned officer. Plus, we need someone out of the battle to help make a way for the Skipper when he returns. Arthur and Number One exchanged glances and the first officer knew that, if the FBI operation went west, it might be up to them to stop the Nazi getting on the Spanish ship, where the spy would be protected by their neutrality. He nodded to Fred.

'Alright Mr Braithwaite, let slip the dogs of war!'

Fred grinned, clearly enjoying the prospect. Arthur reached down the side of the chart table.

'Hold on Fred, you might need an advantage,' he held out the Skipper's sea-going cricket bat, which was feared by fisheries inspectors all over the north sea, plus an elk as Arthur recalled.

'It'll be an honour to swing it for Britain, Mr Stainton. Thank you.'

The bat looked tiny in his meaty paw.

Number One followed Fred down, shaking his head.

Arthur hit the tannoy toggle, 'All hands on deck, please. Free entertainment.'

Chapter Nineteen

43° 39' 29" N, 70° 15' 30"

Portland, Maine

As the lads walked up the wharf, leaving Billy to defend the brow, Arthur stepped through the port-side door at the back of the wheelhouse. Opening the steam steering space, he took one of the Lee Enfield rifles from their homemade rack. Nominally, they were for sinking mines, but Arthur knew they had more rifles than other trawlers because of their work for McDonald. He had been the best shot during training and his rifle had his initials scored onto the stock because it was zeroed for him, i.e. the sights were set for Arthur's use only, so he could be confident he would hit what he aimed at. The magazine held ten rounds, but Arthur usually loaded one clip of five. He could pick up an extra clip or two from the box in the steering space if he thought he'd need them.

He unclipped the magazine and slid the five brass casings with their copper-alloy sheathed projectiles backward to free them from the magazine, and popped them in his pocket. If he was to intimidate people with an unloaded rifle, he didn't want to risk working the bolt out of habit and killing someone!

He decided to go up to the flying bridge, so he had a better view. Once settled, he turned on the small searchlight and pointed it down at the wharf side so anyone approaching the boards they had put across would be blinded, but visible to Arthur and Billy.

Some of White Nab's crew had shoved a way through on the far side of the wharf, and the lads were slowly pushing the Spaniards back. Once they had made around four feet, they stopped, but started trying to make conversation with their opposite numbers.

Arthur flipped up the rear leaf sight and set it for two hundred yards. Might as well look convincing, he reasoned.

The Skipper's lungs were most definitely burning now, every breath was a struggle. He didn't see which way Willow had gone as they turned onto Fore Street and had to slow until he spotted Willow to his right. It had cost him a few paces, but at least he still had him in sight.

A few seconds later, he heard sirens at the junction ahead, and Willow skidded left into Custom House Street. His foot slipped on the paver blocks of the road and the Skipper had made up those few yards he'd just lost. The street was short and suddenly they were crossing the railway tracks and Willow was heading right. The Skipper realised they were on the waterfront, but was pushing himself even harder. He knew all he had to do was push Willow, and he'd fall. But he couldn't make more than a couple of yards on the man before his heart was pounding painfully, and he started falling back. He wasn't sure how many wharves they had passed, but suddenly, Willow careered left and the buildings opposite were flashing, so either the police or FBI had arrived. Turning hard, he felt his ankle twist as he lost footing. He tasted bile as he realised Willow would reach the Spaniard before he could stop him, so he stopped, took two deep breaths and shouted.

'STOP HIM LADS!' he yelled, before limping onward. Suddenly he was overtaken by FBI men and police officers, they had taken up the shouts of 'Stop him!'

Fred could hear sirens to his right and knew the time was now. Shouting 'Have 'em lads!' he waded forward, swinging the Skipper's bat with gusto. He was careful to keep the blows to torso, arms, or legs. Head height might kill someone and he'd heard bad things about American jails.

The lads took up the cry and were punching, pushing, and kicking. The fighting stuttered to a halt, though it was universally agreed that Fred was the last to cease swinging.

Suddenly, they were all blinded.

Up on the flying bridge, Arthur had heard the yells of 'stop him' and swung the searchlight further up the wharf. He could clearly see the Skipper limping and an advancing herd of police and, presumably, FBI overtaking him. As his eyes grew accustomed to the glare, he saw Willow, dark-haired and way in front.

He knew they had lost, Willow was too far ahead. So, Arthur made a decision: he yanked the rifle bolt up and back. There was no time to fill the magazine, he simply pushed a round into the breach and whacked the bolt forward and down. Thumbing off the safety, he put his forearm on the rail and took two slow breaths; on the second exhale he held his breathing, lined up the foresight with the hole in the leaf sight and swung the sights slowly up Willows flailing body. When he judged the range was right, he took up the first trigger pressure, then very gently squeezed before breathing in. His ears rang from the noise and he worked the bolt, beginning to insert another round. Looking over the rail, he realised there was no need. A line of police were between the crumpled man on the floor and the Spanish crew, but the officers were superfluous: the Spaniards had nearly all turned and started walking back to their ship. The Skipper knelt next to Willow's body, and was pulling a satchel from Willow's arm. Bernstein was walking up behind, shaking his head it appeared. Arthur felt his stomach clench, had he done the right thing?

Down on the wharf, Fred was making sure that White Nab's crew were toeing the line and doing nothing to antagonise the authorities. He asked Davy Roxby, one of the deckhands, to quietly take the Skipper's bat back onboard and tell Arthur not to come ashore. He then started saying, gently but firmly, 'Alright lads, the fun's over. Everyone back on board and let these gentlemen do their work.'

Slowly, the tension diffused, and Fred worked to gently disengage the last couple of their lads to reinforce that they were helping the police. He didn't want anyone locked up overnight if he could help it. As luck would have it, he was successful. There were still two Spaniards who were stabbing their fingers at the police. He thought they were only protesting their innocence but were so animated, the police were wary.

At the back of the scrummage, Bernstein walked up to the Skipper, 'What the hell Skipper, I mean, really?'

The Skipper turned, saw Bernstein's eyeline, and laughed, 'Oh, no sir, he's not dead. It's just that I told him my sharpshooter is still aiming at him and he definitely *will* be dead if he moves. Joking aside though, I'd better get back to Captain McDonald, he is injured.'

Bernstein squared up in front of the Skipper, 'I know that Mr Hurton...' the Skipper began to bridle, but Bernstein stepped aside, 'He bled all over my command car so I know damn well he's injured!'

Behind Bernstein, McDonald limped forward, his left shoulder and chest swathed in bandages, 'Buggered up a damn fine coat and suit though. Shame the Nazi survived.'

The Skipper sagged with relief.

Bernstein waved to an ambulance crew who had just pulled up, pointing to Willow. The Skipper whispered, 'Gunshot wound, left shoulder small entry and exit wounds so likely no major damage. That said, I'd get them to stop him bleeding if you want to get anything out of him.'

Bernstein shook his head, 'Skipper, you are a goddamn force of nature.'

The Skipper shook his head, 'Not really sir, but I do have a good malt onboard if you'd like to join us?'

'Sure, but let me organise my guys first. I'll get some men to go with Willow to the hospital. I'll be with you in ten.'

Chapter Twenty

43° 39' 29" N, 70° 15' 30"

Portland, Maine

Back onboard, McDonald winced as he sat back in the Skipper's cabin.

'I'm fine, Skipper. They stitched me up and dressed the wound, nothing major hit, but they recommend I have it checked soon. I imagine I'll need to get to the naval hospital in Halifax fairly briskly.'

'But won't we be questioned here before we can go, sir?'

'No Skipper, you and your crew have just handed the FBI a major intelligence asset and they won't want us British claiming credit. Nor would we want it, of course, lest anyone question American neutrality. See how it works?'

The Skipper smiled, 'I do, sir. If I'd known we have immunity, I'd have filled the bilge with cases of bourbon!'

McDonald was shaking his head as Arthur came in,

looking pensive. 'Here's the hero of the hour!' McDonald yelled, reaching out to pump Arthur's hand, wincing as he did so.

Arthur smiled, looking shaky, 'I thought I'd missed and killed him to be honest.'

McDonald's eyes widened, 'You're not telling me you were aiming for his shoulder are you?'

The Skipper intervened, 'I once saw Arthur bring down a partridge with his son's catapult and a stone, sir. If he says he meant to wing Willow, I wouldn't doubt him.' He winked as he leaned to look at Arthur from behind McDonald's back.

Arthur met McDonald's eyes, 'Well, I did take something of a risk, but my rifle is zeroed, and at two hundred yards I was fairly confident I could put it high on his chest. I just thought it was better to stop him than see him get away with his loot on the freighter.'

The Skipper was biting his knuckle, trying not to laugh, 'Arthur, would you grab the Laphroaig bottle please? I'm just going to get a cold compress on my ankle.'

As the Skipper called up to ask Fred to pop down with a bandage and pad, Arthur asked McDonald what had happened.

'Well, I got stabbed, then strangled, then I stabbed the strangler, and the Skipper ran a marathon before you shot the Nazi bugger and Mr Bernstein took him for interrogation. I think they're the key facts, eh, Skipper?'

'Spot on, Sir.'

Arthur chuckled as he set down the bottle and four

glasses. The Skipper frowned as he looked at the swelling around Fred's right eye socket.

'Have you been in the wars Fred?' He nodded at the bruise as he handed the big man a glass of malt.

'No Skipper, just a bit of fun. Cheeky bugger threw a shackle at me. The result of which is another dent in your sea-going bat, I'm sorry to say.'

'As long as it's back on board and in one piece Fred.'

'Oh aye, Skipper. I washed the blood off it and everything. As good as new. Here, let me get this compress on for you.'

They were all laughing as the door opened and Number One entered, with Bernstein descending the steps behind him.

'Having a party, Skipper?' he beamed.

Fred glanced up as he tied off the bandage, 'Keep it tight Skipper, it'll hold off the swelling.' Looking around the room he spoke again, 'The lads were trojans tonight Skipper, permission to splice the mainbrace?'

'Of course, Fred. Just a tot, though. I suspect we might be going to sea shortly.'

Bernstein's voice floated through from the passage, 'Let 'em have a decent slug of rum, Skipper. We'll have the wharf sealed off until morning.'

The Skipper looked up, 'You heard the gentleman, Fred. Thank the lads from me and give them a decent tot.'

'Thanks Skipper.' Fred was squeezing around Bernstein at the bottom of the wheelhouse steps.

The Skipper gestured Arthur to get in beside him as

he shuffled round the settee and sat behind the table. McDonald squeezed in at the other side, and Number One gestured to Bernstein to take the last seat.

'As I was only supporting Fred in a brawl, meaning I did nothing, I feel you fellows deserve the seat, sir!'

Bernstein smiled, 'Thank you; much appreciated,' he shed his overcoat and shimmied himself in.

Number One took another glass from the Skipper's wardrobe and put it on the table while the Skipper poured them all a hefty measure. Putting the bottle down, he lifted his glass.

'To victory!'

They lifted their arms as one, 'Victory!'

Bernstein smacked his lips as he tasted the smoky velvet of the whisky.

'Well, gentlemen, I think it all worked out OK. Horace, I've spoken with Jack McDaid and he's delighted with the outcome, but what of the magnetron?'

McDonald smiled, reaching under the table and placed a waxed cardboard box on the table. He took off the lid and placed a palm sized device on the table. It had a pole connector on a screw fitting, then circular sets of metal vanes painted black. Two tubes projected from top of the circular centre section, each of which had a glass bulb from which protruded pins, onto which were soldered loops of braided copper wire.

'This, gentlemen, may win the war for us. I can't go into detail, but it really is that important. Everyone in this room, as well as the FBI personnel and police force, not to forget the Royal Canadian Mounted Police, helped to prevent this getting back to the Nazis. I should also say, Eli, that the serial number agrees with the information Sir Henry Tizard's people gave me.'

He carefully repackaged it, fitting a protective tube over the protruding parts and placed it between two wooden formers in the box.

Bernstein smiled, 'Looks like we all got that we wanted gentlemen. The early impression is that Willow, who still says his real name is Joachim Grüber, will give up his network, but we shall see. In any event, we have rolled up the existing elements of at least a part of it. Galling though it is, we may have to let him go to a new life and identity if he gives up the information. He has already indicated that it was he who executed his colleague Kurt Halsted, because he was out of control.'

McDonald nodded, 'So what about us, Eli?'

Bernstein grinned, 'As I mentioned, I have spoken with Jack, and he thinks the best way forward is to put out a press release to the effect that the FBI have been involved in a joint operation with field offices and police forces and have arrested one man, with another one dead. Shots were fired on Long Wharf, and the arrested man is being questioned. We cleaned up and got the second guy away before anyone showed any interest, so the public only know of an incident on the wharf.'

'That sounds nice and neat,' said McDonald, smiling.

Bernstein met his eyes, 'Yeah, it is. I convinced Jack it's the best solution to maintain our neutrality. On that subject, he has suggested you guys head out for Halifax early tomorrow. We will deal with the Spanish vessel, but best there isn't a white ensign flying in the background of any press photographs. I'll fly up in a couple of days and we'll do a wrap up. Are you OK to travel, Horace? I hadn't thought to ask.'

'Yes, I'm fine, they have me some strong pills. As regards us disappearing, I fully expected that, Eli. It's the best plan.'

Bernstein rose, 'I'd better go back to the interrogation now, but before I go, I want to thank everyone in this room for their contribution, but especially Captain McDonald, our athlete, Skipper Hurton, and the sniper, Mr Stainton. Horace, I'll get young Will to sanitise our office and drop anything of yours off here before he goes for shuteye. See you all in Halifax.' His eyes crinkled as he lurched for the door: the Skipper had just lit his pipe.

At 04:00 they had steam up and were ready to leave. It was dark, and a fine drizzle blew across the deck as they let go and went astern. A light came on within the Spaniard's bridge and was quickly extinguished. The Skipper wondered what would happen to the ship and crew.

Once past the promontory at the south end of Cushing

Island, they steered east-southeast. The wind was fresh from the northeast and a swell was building, so the Skipper wanted to get into deep water as quickly as possible. The breeze was full of sleet and visibility was variable. They altered to due east once past buoy number two, so they had a good northing from Three Dory Ridge. He suspected the local lads could cut it finer, but he was always inclined to be pessimistic, a slightly higher coal bill was better than a salvage operation as his father, T'owd Skipper, had always said. He wasn't sure how fast the low pressure system was moving, but he'd laid off a course to give a good offing south of Seal Island and the shoals on the southeast coast of Newfoundland before heading east for a while and standing well out from the east coast. Like all sensible sailors, he feared a lee shore. Even though he knew the low would move away eastward, he didn't know when. He'd gauge the weather once they were ready to turn up the coast of Newfoundland and head up to Halifax.

Once they were in deeper water, he handed over to Arthur, with Fred at the wheel, and went below. Arthur had suggested Number One take the forenoon watch to give the Skipper's ankle some time to heal. The Skipper accepted, but they all knew he'd be back up well before that to check the weather and their progress.

McDonald was in Number One's cabin and Billy popped down every so often to check if he needed anything. He was in a fair bit of pain and his shoulder had stiffened, but he could cope. He recited 'Invictus' in his head and certainly felt bloody, but unbowed. As he fitfully drifted in and out of sleep, he was warmed by the knowledge that the magnetron was inside its box in Number One's locker.

As expected, the Skipper reappeared just before the end of the morning watch. Number One was already in the wheelhouse, preparing for his forenoon hitch between eight and midday.

'Due south of the Ram Island light, Skipper. Distance just under 15 miles from the light. Around 34 miles run but the last half is dead reckoning, so I've drawn a circle of uncertainty around my position mark. Seal Island light is visible for thirty-one miles so we can get a better fix and adjust our course as soon as we can see it.'

The Skipper nodded, 'Well done chaps,' peering forward, he could see very little through the Kent clear view screen apart from flying snow and mist but the motion had eased, 'Is the motion a result of deeper water or is the wind easing, Arthur?'

'I think it's a bit of both, Skipper. Also, next time we get the opportunity, we should let the lookouts have some sealskin gloves, like the ones they had in Norway. Oh, and I've had the lifelines rigged across the well to the gun and whaleback, and a jackstay either side of the deckhouse.'

The Skipper began pulling on his oilskin and sou'wester, 'I'll try it out Arthur, I'm just going to check how Captain McDonald is doing. If he's asleep, I'll leave him be. I need to stretch my legs and see how my ankle will hold up. I won't be long.'

Five minutes later, the skipper was descending the steps to the aft cabin. Entering, he turned to his left and gently knocked on the door of the cabin. A voice answered, 'Hello? Come in,' so he opened the door and entered. McDonald looked pale but seemed in good spirits.

'Hello Skipper, been doing some sunbathing, have you?' He nodded at the dripping oilskins.

'Until I saw Arthur in a grass skirt, sir. Then I came in here to shelter from the sight!'

McDonald smiled, 'Sounds a bit brisk out there, everything alright?'

'Oh yes. The ankle's holding up well and we're on track at the moment, despite poor visibility. This weather should abate through today, but there could be a swell for a while after it eases. We'll be able to make better time then. Unfortunately, it'll still be the best part of two days for the whole passage.'

'Shouldn't matter. I'm reasonably comfortable in here. The police surgeon said the blade hit nothing vital, and I had a look earlier, just eased up the padded bandage and all looks well, no sign of infection. The quack said there may be a bit of nerve damage, but it's painful, not life threatening.'

The Skipper nodded, 'Get a couple of hours' sleep if you can, Billy usually gets some bacon in before we leave port and you won't want to miss his bacon and mushroom rolls!'

McDonald's eyes were drooping as he laid back with a wave.

Stopping to ask Billy to keep an eye on McDonald, the

Skipper made his way forward. He bade Number One a quiet watch and went to his cabin. He was asleep within a minute of laying his head down.

Chapter Twenty-One

44° 35′ 09″ N, 63° 29′ 14″

Halifax, Nova Scotia

Two days had passed and the Skipper sat by McDonald's bed in the naval hospital. The surgeon was speaking to McDonald about the surgery he'd carried out a few hours earlier and it seemed all had gone well.

Once the doctor had gone, McDonald pushed himself up in the bed.

'I don't mind admitting, Skipper, that I'm getting a bit of cabin fever. There is some good news, however; Bernstein is on his way north as we speak, so we should get a full debrief in the next twenty-four hours.'

The Skipper nodded, 'Good news, sir. What is the story with the item? We are onboard all the time, but it still makes me nervous. The enemy did seem keen on getting hold of it.'

'Yes, they were, rather. As I understand it, from the officer commanding this base, someone from the Tizard Mission will be retrieving it in the next day or two. Now, I've had a message from my boss, Sir Peter; he is keen on me travelling home with you because he doesn't want any records of me travelling by air. Not that it really matters, it's just he wants to preserve as much deniability for the Americans as possible. I also suspect that he may be punishing me ever so slightly for being, shall we say, unsubtle. The joke's entirely on him if that is the case, because I'd rather travel with you, given all the luxury liners are now troop-ships!'

'We'll save the stateroom for you. Not a problem at all.'

McDonald shook his head, 'I'm strictly steerage old chap, I know my place!'

The Skipper suddenly laughed, 'Svein is in heaven, by the way. The fireboxes are cooling and he's emptying the ash-pits, catching up on routine maintenance and is positively bubbling that he can properly clean the boiler while we wait! I can tell you, if there's a blue riband for trawlers, it's as good as ours.'

The Skipper and McDonald both had that sudden drop off which hospital visitors inevitably face. The 'what do I say next' moment. McDonald cleared his throat but was saved by a brisk lady in nurse's uniform asking if he could manage lunch.

McDonald peered at her, 'My dear, I am ravenous!'

The nurse glared pointedly at the Skipper, who stood up. She wasn't as fearsome as Mavis, but definitely from the same mould. As he pulled on his coat, his jaw dropped open.

'I'm going to get somebody to stab me sir. Right away,' he pointed at the plate, 'two eggs; with Spam! I've not seen the like for over a year!'

The nurse shook her head, 'Self-inflicted injuries only get bread and water, sadly. Now kindly let Captain McDonald eat!'

The Skipper saluted her as he left.

Twenty-four hours later, they sat in a small consulting room which they had borrowed. McDonald beamed at Bernstein and the Skipper from the padded chair behind the desk.

'What's the news then, Eli?'

Bernstein took a deep breath, 'Well, where do I start? Let's deal with The Spaniard first. We've let him go, however, I had a private chat with the skipper and first officer before they left. I made it clear that, if we hear so much as a whisper about the Nazi spy, then we will immediately release a notice to the press that a brave Spanish freighter captain turned in the German because he disagrees with spying on neutral powers. The press notice will also mention that we gave him a significant reward in recognition of his bravery in defying his government and the Nazi dictatorship. I said that we'd name the ship just to make absolutely sure that either General Franco or the SD got the right man. We fed him the legend that he waited for a long time, but then the man he'd been waiting for turned up and said that the operation was off, and that he should leave.'

McDonald nodded, 'That'll hold him, Eli. He'll be on tenterhooks for a few months, though! I wouldn't like to be in his shoes.'

'Yeah, that's what we thought! Now, we backtracked the guy who tried to strangle you. Turns out that he'd flown up from Washington and the operational office down there is working on finding out who he is and who he associates with. That might give us a potential route into other parts of the network. We do know that he was to take something to Spain, then return. As to our friend Joachim; once we pointed out that he is absolutely on his own, and there isn't a soul on the other side of the Atlantic with even a slight suspicion of what happened to him, why, then he became positively friendly. We now have the entire network, from the guy that you told us about Horace, down to Grüber's level. We are currently building a back story, such that he can emerge in a few days with a plausible tale, and some proof, which we will fabricate of course. Essentially, the story will be that the guy you killed went bad, and betrayed the operation to the Americans. He tried to persuade Grüber to flee with him, so Grüber stabbed him to death. If they buy it, then we can start running him to get disinformation over there, if they don't buy it, then he'll just have to be given a more thorough debrief and then allowed to disappear. I can also tell you we have removed your names from our records, so this was purely an FBI operation.'

McDonald beamed, 'I am really pleased for you, Eli. None of this would've happened without you... and the man who just walked through that door!'

They all turned to see André Bouchard beaming as he strode across the ward. He sat on the end of the bed, and from his raincoat pocket, pulled a bottle of rye whiskey.

'With best regards from Canada, Horace!' His voice boomed out.

McDonald paled, 'My God, man! What are you thinking of, the matron here makes Adolf Hitler look positively jovial. Hide it in the name of all that's holy!'

The Skipper took a theatrical look around as Bouchard belly laughed.

'It's good to see you kept a sense of humour, eh?'

McDonald's eyes gleamed as he realised the Skipper was staring around the ward and had pushed a hip flask into his hand, 'Quick, sir. The enemy might return at any moment!'

The fates were against the Skipper, however, because the Matron reappeared just as the hip flask returned to his hand.

'Bugger, just my luck.'

The Matron shot a steely glance into the consulting room and shook her head.

Bernstein stood, 'Sorry guys but I have to get back, I'm ordered to be there when your First Officer hands over the cutlery to the guys from the Mission. I guess Jack is emphasising that the US has played its part. When I get back, Jack wants me scouring the airwaves and diplomatic communiques for anything that proves they've bought the story, just as soon as Grüber sends his message. I'll be here for a couple of days, but no more.'

McDonald looked around his bed, realising how close he felt to this team. He knew that war is war and however much he respected and liked them, they would all have to follow their own roads, doing whatever became necessary to protect their own countries, and win the war. In his heart was certain that, despite the harsh realities of war, respect, friendship and comradeship were the glue that held alliances together. He felt he finally understood why Churchill was so devoted to the idea that the United States must join the struggle. Britain had shown, with great courage and fortitude, that it could defend its own shores and show the Nazis weren't invincible, but to push them back and free Europe would need more than Britain, its empire, and the Commonwealth could give.

Number One and Bernstein shook hands with the representative of the Tizard Mission as flurries of sleet swirled around the dockside.

'Thank you, gentlemen. I don't know how you did it, but it feels miraculous that the magnetron was recovered. Sir Henry knows nothing about the theft and replacement of the magnetron, and once we swap this with the replacement, he need never know what happened here.

Sir Peter has been in touch and asked us to keep this on a need to know basis because SIS operations in the United States might raise issues about their neutrality and present problems for President Roosevelt in the imminent presidential election. I find it sad that your achievement will never become public.'

Number One shook his head, 'Thank you for your kind words, sir, but we're not in this for public acclamation, we just want to win this damned war!'

Bernstein shrugged, 'We are neutral, but I suspect that won't be the case for too long. So, yes, I agree with Piers entirely!'

Shaking their hands, the Tizard man turned back to his MI5 escorts and walked off to their car.

The next day, the Skipper was in the wheelhouse. He had taken out his North Atlantic route-planning chart and was looking in his various sailing directions for weather predictions and sea ice extents. He wanted to be ahead of the game, because it was clear their next voyage would be eastwards, across the great grey Atlantic.

Glancing down at the quay, it amazed him to see Captain McDonald and Special Agent in Charge Bernstein walking towards his ship. The Skipper went quickly down to deck level and welcomed his visitors aboard. He noticed Bernstein carried a canvas holdall.

'Welcome onboard gentlemen, to what do I owe this

pleasure?'

McDonald grinned, 'Oh, we were missing the nautical life terribly skipper!'

Shaking his head, the Skipper suggested they go down to the aft cabin so there were fewer ladders or steps for Captain McDonald to negotiate. Once settled, they placed a coffee order with Billy, and the Skipper looked quizzically around the table.

Bernstein laughed, 'Don't worry, Skipper, we won't ask you to run any more marathons! So, my boss has had some people keeping a cap on the press reports in Portland, interest has mostly waned, but it does seem that one enterprising young reporter is still sniffing around the events of that night. Now, fouling up the presidential election is probably uppermost in Jack's mind, but he wants to draw a line under that night once and for all. To prevent the young hack from pulling any threads which could unravel our cover story, your Admiralty has reluctantly agreed to confirm, if asked, that you were at sea as a convoy escort when the events of that night took place. Captain McDonald did some browbeating and his surgeon has discharged him, so he can travel with you as ordered. Your people will contact you shortly, but we understand you are to join a HX convoy going to Liverpool as an escort. We understand the convoy leaves tomorrow. Apparently, they had already beefed up the escort after the debacle of HX.79, so the convoy should be well defended. Just think, you'll be able to tell your grandkids that you were asked to leave North America by the FBI!'

'I don't need to add further notoriety to my reputation, thank you, Mr Bernstein!'

There was a knock at the door and Arthur dropped in an envelope for the Skipper.

'Hang on Arthur, would you?'

The Skipper opened the envelope and read his typed orders, 'We are to join convoy HX.86, leaving Halifax at 13:00 tomorrow, as anti submarine escort. I am to meet with the Captain of HMS Voltaire, which is an armed merchant cruiser, for a briefing in about an hour from now. Arthur, get Number One and the rest of the crew to gather in the ship's well. We need to give them a pep talk before we sail. We've had a fine holiday, but they need to get their wartime faces back on as of now. While I'm with Voltaire's man, I'd like yourself and Number One to check everything one last time and give the lads some gun and depth charge drills. Safety at all times, I don't want the bloody stern blown off!'

McDonald could see the Skipper's mind racing and marvelled at how he could change tack without pausing for breath.

Bernstein shook their hands, 'I'll come down to wave you off in the morning if I can. If not, then godspeed and I hope to meet you all again once the Nazis are beaten, who knows?'

McDonald shook his hand, 'If not before, dear boy, if not before.'

The following morning, the weather was dry, but very grey and breezy. As the deckhands made final preparations for leaving, a Canadian naval rating, with a pronounced limp, passed over some mail for Captain McDonald.

McDonald leafed through it and all were routine and mostly out of date by now. The last one, however, was a stunner. It was from Janet Hopkins, the young woman from the British Security Coordination who had dropped in the signal decrypt at Portland. The letter was brief:

Dear Horace, I changed my mind. My address and telephone number are on the enclosed card, and I'm told I am to be reassigned to Blighty come the middle of next year. I look forward to hearing from you soon.

Kindest regards

Janet

McDonald felt warm despite the breeze and shoved the card and letter into the inside pocket of his jacket before re-buttoning the heavy duffel coat Arthur had given him.

An hour later the shore lines were cast off and white Nab was easing out of her berth. The Skipper was on the bridge deck making sure they were clear when McDonald nudged him and pointed.

Eli Berstein stood on the quayside, leaning into the wind. He saw them, turned and raised an arm, waving back and forth twice, before turning and walking away. Without a word, they both turned to look over the bow, forward to who knew what.

Chapter Twenty-Two

42° 08' 55" N, 56° 20' 53" W

North Atlantic, Two Days Out from Halifax

The Skipper was scraping out his pipe bowl prior to refilling, while Captain McDonald looked around at the view through the windows, stunned.

Great grey walls of water with white foam trails, like the tracks of rivers running down their advancing faces, came one after another from ahead. White Nab rose, cut the water on the crest, then fell into the trough, where her bow slammed the grey-green water and spread two sheets of white spray from the bows, with some flowing over the whaleback before diverting, mostly, over the side before she lifted for the next sea. As she rose, McDonald realised he was looking upwards at the top of the next wave, with a dry mouth.

The Skipper coughed.

'I've looked at the weather forecast, sir. I'd make the most of this if I were you. It's likely to get a bit lumpy later on.'
'Bugger off, Skipper. There's a good chap.'

THE END

If you enjoyed this book then, first of all , thank you! If you'd like to hear about future work and news, then please subscribe to my monthly newsletter by clicking or copying this link
https://subscribepage.io/zMC2Ri
Every subscriber is sent a link to download the free eBook version of The Skipper's First War, charting his formative experiences in World War One.
The following pages are the introduction to the next book in the series, 'The Skipper's Winter' I hope you enjoy reading these books as much as I do writing them!

Chapter One

57° 51' 42" N, 05° 18' 35" W

'Patrol Base 8' near Badcaul

The mountains around Little Loch Broom shone in the pale sunshine; the white of the snow reflecting the pale blue of the sky.

The beauty was breathtaking, the air cold and clean. This was the Skipper's idea of heaven.

Arthur had the lads over the side, chipping, wire brushing, and repainting rust streaks; a legacy of their recent trip over the Atlantic and back. He liked to keep His Majesty's Trawler 'White Nab' as tidy as possible.

Their return from Halifax had been mercifully quiet. This had been unexpected, given the mauling which their outbound convoy had received. The Skipper had been told that either the u-boats attacked as a pack and caused mayhem, or the convoy was uneventful. There seem to be no middle ground.

Having spent a wonderful three days at their homes in Scarborough, a seaside town and harbour in the north riding of Yorkshire, they were not best pleased to be recalled to Patrol Base Eight, a secret location on the west coast of Scotland for vessels seconded from the Royal Naval Patrol Service, whose purpose it was to assist the Secret Intelligence Service, supporting them in their clandestine work.

The eccentric Captain Stevenson ran the unit, and it was he who was walking toward the Skipper, a small cigar hanging from his mouth.

'Morning Skipper,' he said, a spray of cigar ash accompanying his words.

The Skipper smiled, 'Morning, sir. I hope you're well?'

Captain Stevenson waved, 'Let's stroll up to my seaside residence, shall we? We can talk in there.'

The Skipper felt they could talk pretty much anywhere within five miles of this base, with no risk of being overheard. The beauty and isolation were its main selling points as far as he was concerned. But he knew that Captain Stevenson's seaside residence, his own name for the moss covered shack, which had been just about the only building on the site before Nissen Huts had arrived, and the base had grown into a base for SIS naval assets.

Assets, in the plural, might have been stretching it before they had left for the United States, since White Nab was their first and, at that time, only vessel. Now, he noticed there was a small Lowestoft steam drifter moored up at a buoy further up the loch. Unlike White Nab, the drifter was still in full civilian trim. It made sense, she could probably go anywhere and pass for a local fishing boat.

Stevenson had spotted him looking, 'Our newest recruit, Skipper. Her crew are doing their sneaky beaky training in the highlands at the moment. You'll meet them in due course, and I think you'll get on very well.

Inside Stevenson's shack, they had filled the little iron stove with dried peat blocks, and the interior was wonderfully warm, as well as smelling marvellous.

'Cigar, Skipper?'

'Yes please, sir, if you don't mind.'

'Not at all dear boy,' he offered the open pack over to the Skipper.

The Skipper's match rasped and flared as he prepared to light his cigar. It tasted smooth, without the flavour of his Pudsey Naval Blend tobacco. He was a habitual pipe smoker and always bought his 'baccy' in bulk from the importer in Leeds.

The Skipper turned as the door handle rattled.

Captain Horace McDonald, who was both his boss and a man he considered a friend, walked in and shook their hands.

'Hello to both of you, it's great to see you. Skipper, I'm so sorry about cutting your leave short, but I'm sure you'll understand why it was necessary after I explain what we are planning.'

The Skipper felt a certain hollowness in the pit of his stomach. This sounded like another mission. He managed a smile, 'I'll take your word, sir.'

'Missing your good lady already, Skipper?'

'No, sir. Just terrified that she won't have forgiven me by the time we get back. Which, unless it's a two-year mission, is fairly likely!'

Stevenson and McDonald chuckled.

'Your Mavis adores you, Skipper. You know that! Anyway, shall we get down to business?'

He glanced around the room, thinking that nobody would object to getting down to business if there was a malt afterward.

'Well, we're back to scientists, again I'm afraid, Skipper. This time, Finnish scientists. One of our chaps at Cambridge has been working in a field of science, which we feel is critically important. I will not tell a lie, it's the same field as the man you extracted from Slyngøya Island, so you know how vital it is.'

The Skipper nodded, and Stevenson's eyes slid over toward him. The older man gave him look which was almost pity, but which the Skipper didn't notice.

McDonald continued, 'Well, these chaps have expressed an interest in becoming involved in research, either in Britain or the United States. The problem we have is that their government isn't awfully keen to let them go. Now we dispatched someone to speak to them, one of our chaps you understand. On his return, he was concerned. He felt quite strongly that they were being watched. Who precisely was doing the watching is uncertain, but given what we know, it's most likely to be their own government. In the time it took our man to return home and make his report, the situation over there developed. Our chap was clearly correct: they must have been under surveillance, and he'd told them what he suspected, asking them to be careful. So the next thing we hear is that they've both disappeared. A couple of days ago, we heard from the Norwegian resistance that they are in hiding, and currently safe. The resistance people think that the best option is a plan to extract them quickly and quietly from somewhere in the far north, but not too close to the Russian border until we know which side the communists are on.'

'Have you any suggestions, sir?'

'Well, the resistance tell us they can get the scientists to Honningvåg and there's a beach to the north which might be suitable for getting them off. Now, one of our chaps holidayed in the Finnmark and doesn't recall a beach, so we've asked the RAF to send a photo reconnaissance aircraft over there, but they're sniffy about the range. The maps and charts we have suggest there is a rocky cove which is available anytime over half-tide but will need a boat, maybe an inflatable as you used on Slyngøya the first time. We'd ask the resistance if they can send a photo, but we are running out of time. Any initial thoughts, Skipper?'

The Skipper rubbed his chin, 'I'd say we'll need to do some careful passage planning, sir. I think an approach from the north would be advisable, given the Kriegsmarine seem to own the west coast. Let's see what we can do!'

Captain Stevenson seemed to close his eyes in fear. An expression the Skipper did notice...

Printed in Great Britain
by Amazon